P9-BZM-832

PENGUIN CRIME FICTION

THE KENTISH MANOR MURDERS

Julian Symons is a most celebrated practitioner of the crime novel (*The Color of Murder* and *The Progress of a Crime* both received awards as best mystery of the year), and he is recognized as one of the great British experts on the genre. His history of the form, *Bloody Murder* (Viking, 1985), was called by Len Deighton "the classic study of crime in fiction." In 1976 Mr. Symons succeeded Agatha Christie as president of Britain's Detection Club and in 1977 he was made a Grand Master of the Swedish Academy of Detection. In 1982 he was named a Grand Master of the Mystery Writers of America, an honor accorded to only three other English writers—Graham Greene, Eric Ambler, and Daphne du Maurier.

Mr. Symons has been equally successful as a critic, social and military historian, and biographer (of Charles Dickens, Thomas Carlyle, and Edgar Allan Poe). He lives in Kent near the sea.

THE
KENTISH MANOR
MURDERS

Julian Symons

PENGUIN BOOKS

PENGUIN BOOKS
Published by the Penguin Group
Viking Penguin, a division of Penguin Books USA Inc.,
40 West 23rd Street,
New York, New York 10010, U.S.A.
Penguin Books Ltd, 27 Wrights Lane,
London W8 5TZ, England
Penguin Books Australia Ltd, Ringwood,
Victoria, Australia
Penguin Books Canada Ltd, 2801 John Street,
Markham, Ontario, Canada L3R 1B4
Penguin Books (N.Z.) Ltd, 182-190 Wairau Road,
Auckland 10, New Zealand

Penguin Books Ltd, Registered Offices:
Harmondsworth, Middlesex, England

First published in Great Britain by Macmillan London Ltd 1988
First published in the United States of America
by Viking Penguin, a division of Penguin Books USA Inc., 1988
Published in Penguin Books 1989

1 3 5 7 9 10 8 6 4 2

LIBRARY OF CONGRESS CATALOGING IN PUBLICATION DATA
Symons, Julian, 1912–
The Kentish manor murders/ Julian Symons.
p.   cm. — (Penguin crime fiction)
ISBN 0 14 01.08726
I. Title.
[PR6037.Y5K36   1989]
823′.912—dc19   88–37998

Printed in the United States of America
Set in Plantin

Contents

Prelude   Cologne, May   7

1. The Enthusiasm of Desmond O'Malley   15

2. Castle Baskerville   21

3. Unexpected Meeting with an Old Friend   47

4. The Manuscript   57

5. Farewell, Desdemona   65

6. Marty Clayton's Story   75

7. The Man in Amsterdam   83

8. The Raid   101

9. At Castle Baskerville   113

10. People in London   127

11. Wednesday   141

12. Thursday and Friday   153

Afterwards   187

Prelude

The place was called Café Exotica, and looked like a gigantic greenhouse. It had been built out over the Rhine, the glass walls supported by the thinnest of metal struts, so that wherever you sat you could look at the river. The roof also was glazed, and the greenhouse effect was enhanced by dozens of potted plants standing around the entrance and between tables. The café was a brasserie with a floor show, or a cabaret where you could eat and drink. On a warm day it became intensely hot, and this had been a warm day. With windows and roof open as they were on this evening it was difficult to hear the performers who sang or told dirty jokes, but few people listened to them. The Exotica was a place where people came to talk about what was new in the theatre or film, journalism, gambling or crime, not to listen to third-rate singers or fourth-rate comics.

The tables were painted green and had marble tops, the chairs were green with plush seats. Three men sat at one table, glasses of beer in front of them. One was English, another German. The third man was older than the others and sat a little apart from them. His face was thin, his complexion dark, his nose curved. A mass of white hair rising to a crest made him look like a cockatoo. He was watching the floor show.

They spoke in English, and indeed the Englishman had no other language. He looked now at a gold wrist-watch. 'What time you got?'

The German was thin, pale and sandy. 'Twenty after ten.'

'I say the same, funny coincidence. We both say he's an hour late.'

'Fifty minutes.'

'Fifty minutes, an hour, he's not here. What kind of person is that, eh, this is our first meet and he's not here.'

'He is a busy man. He will be here.'

'You think we're not, you think we got nothing better to do than sit round in this poncey place waiting for a geezer so busy he's not going to show? Let me remind you, Hans whatever your name is, we don't contact you, it's you who contact us.'

'If you will forgive me, we meet because your people are having some trouble—'

'I'm not so bleeding sure I will forgive you, I'm not in the forgiving business, you want forgiving you've come to the wrong shop, you go to the gent upstairs for that.' The German shook his head to show that he did not understand. 'You spin me this sweet tale about connections, the big man you're like that with, and we both know what we're talking about. We don't ask no favours you don't give any, money is what we're talking about, we give it you get it, right? Or am I wrong, was you suggesting you give us money, was that the proposition?'

The German shook his head again. The man with white hair did not look away from the floor show. He said, 'Jacko.'

'But is that the proposition, or is the idea we hand over our readies on account of this big man who isn't here tonight, but just might be able to show another time, this big man who can do us favours? I'd really like to know if that's the idea, because if it is we can say piss off and we can all get out of this place where the smell turns me up. If I want to be in a jungle I can go up the Amazon, right? But I don't have to be in a jungle, I'm just here to meet this man who can solve any little problems we might be having. I thought you Jerries were hot for punctuality, always on the dot, do everything according to plan, the trains run on time, they tell me you even use a stopwatch in bed.' He laughed, showing a couple of gold teeth. His hair grew low over his forehead, his thick nose had been flattened. He wore a grubby open-neck shirt from which hair sprouted, and jeans.

'Not Cologners.'

'They don't use a stopwatch?'

'They are not punctual. People say when you make an appointment with a Cologner for Friday you should say which week. They like to gamble, take chances, don't worry about tomorrow.' Sweat had gathered on the German's forehead, and he wiped it away. 'I am from Hamburg.'

'Hamburgers or Cologners, you ask me Germans are balloons full of hot air. And they're so rich you can't even give 'em money.'

'Here he is.'

The man who approached them, brushing aside intrusive palm trees and a plant with branches like octopus tentacles, was squarish, almost squat. His face was square, the jaw thrust out prominently, in the middle of the face a snub nose and an unexpected rosebud mouth. His hair was shaven to stubble. His voice was deep, not harsh. He took the fourth chair at the table. 'My apologies. Urgent business.'

The man with white hair turned away from the girl singing barely audible blues songs. The square man said, 'Otto Müller.'

The man with white hair said, 'Oberkommissär Müller. I think you know our names. I have a little of several languages, but Jacko only English. We can talk in English?' Müller nodded. 'In case you're recording this conversation I suggest we speak of business, without defining it in detail. Is that agreed?'

Müller looked amused. 'Agreed.'

'First, this meeting has been called by you.'

'By me? No such thing.'

'I will rephrase it. We have had some little problems recently. Hans got in touch with Jacko here, said he might be able to help us.'

'Better.' Müller caught the arm of a passing waiter. 'Beer.'

'And Hans mentioned your name. So how can you help?'

'I know you, although we have not met. I don't know this man.'

'Jacko makes the arrangements, pays the couriers, knows the dealers. He knows what he's got to do and does it. I'm sure he has no responsibility for any problems.'

Jacko's thick brows had gone up so that they almost reached his mat of hair. 'Thanks for the certificate, *boss*. But you can speak to me, I'm here not fifty bleeding miles away, and I don't appreciate it when you say he knows what he's got to do because at this moment in time he don't like what he's doing, talking to a policeman, and don't know why he's doing it. I don't see any divvy in that at any time, I never knew any good come of a meet with a policeman bent or straight, it gives me the shakes, I feel like I ate something didn't agree with me. And that's an English policeman, I get the cramps as well as the shakes when it's a Jerry copper who could be sussing us out, and especially there's no point in talking to a Jerry copper when we already have—'

'Jacko, you talk too much.' The white-haired man transferred his attention back to the floor show. The blues singer was belting out a refrain about love and fate, but the café was now almost full, and not much of it came through.

'Somebody's got to stop pissing around and say it out loud. We got a deal already, pay good money for it. Now this piss artist Hans comes along and says he's got some kind of say so, he can work bleeding miracles. So I say, what's wrong with the set-up we got already?'

Müller's beer had arrived. He took a long draught of it,

wiped his mouth. 'Cologne Kolsch is best.' Nobody contradicted him. 'It is right to be careful, but I am not wired up, that would be stupid.' He took off his jacket, held up his arms. 'Would you wish to examine?' The white-haired man shook his head.

'Thank you. Now I will reply to the question. You have an arrangement with Inspector Ernst, is that correct? And through Ernst similar arrangements in Belgium, the Netherlands, Scandinavia, perhaps France. Correct?'

Jacko opened his mouth in surprise, closed it again. The white-haired man said, 'Assume it's so. What then?'

'Recently you have trouble, correct? I tell you why. The arrangement is terminated.'

'I don't know what you mean. It is you who have mentioned a name, not me.' He chose his words carefully. 'I will say only that if we had an arrangement it is continuing. So far as we know.' The last words were not exactly a question, but Müller took them as such. His rosebud mouth pursed in a satisfied smirk.

'I said your arrangement is terminated. Ernst is under arrest. He had other arrangements similar to the one with you. Ernst was greedy.'

Hans giggled. Jacko, silenced, looked at the white-haired man. His attention seemed concentrated on the act that had replaced the singer. A thin man, dressed in clothes much too big for him, was trying to do conjuring tricks, all of which failed dismally.

Müller said softly, 'So?'

'What you tell me is not entirely unexpected. We knew something was wrong.'

'There is a new broom in the Police Department. He is determined to sweep away corruption. Ernst had to go, he was too greedy, kept things too much to himself.'

The white-haired man's attention seemed fixed on the inept conjurer's act. The hangdog expression of the stage performer became more marked than ever as he drew a string of sausages out of a top hat instead of the rabbit he had put into it. Müller's rosebud mouth pursed in disapproval. 'I do not interest you?'

'You do, very much.' The white-haired man concentrated attention on the policeman. 'I am not sure why you are telling me this.'

'Hans is an agent of the department. He works closely with me. He is trustworthy.'

'Yes.'

'Ernst was greedy. Also he was not of sufficient importance. It is a mistake to make arrangements with somebody not of sufficient importance.'

'Another arrangement would be possible?'

'I repeat, Hans is trustworthy.'

'That's good news. Let me ask you something. Why are we meeting here? Anybody can see us. You say you know me, so you will know whether we should be seen together. There must be people here who know you, perhaps even the waiter. Why did we not talk privately?'

Müller wagged a playful finger. 'I thought you were more sophisticated. It is the job of a policeman to know everybody, talk to many kinds of people, you understand that. And so long as he does it in public, nobody asks questions. You are right, when I look round here I see a dozen people who know Oberkommissär Müller, actors, journalists, men I have met in the course of business and put away. I shall speak to some of them as I go out, I shall not hide myself. If they recognise you, they will feel no surprise that we should meet and talk. But if we had met in private and been seen – I am sure I need not say more. We shall not meet again, however. The arrangement may be a little different from any you made with Ernst, but Hans will discuss it. That is, of course, if you wish.'

He got up, nodded to the white-haired man, ignored Jacko and Hans and left them, pausing on the way out to talk to people at another table. Afterwards the white-haired man left

Jacko and Hans to argue about the details, while he talked to the owner of the Exotica. On his return he found Jacko alone, full of indignation.

'Would you believe it, you make a straight deal with a bent copper, and another bent copper has him put away and asks for nigh on double, then has the hard neck to call the first one greedy. I tell you what it is, you can't make a straight deal with anyone these days, they're all on the take.' He looked questioningly at his companion. 'You reckon they're on the level? I didn't like that poncey copper. Still, I suppose it wasn't a waste of time.'

'Oh no,' the white-haired man said. 'It wasn't a waste of time.'

This was May. The arrangement worked fairly smoothly until September.

1. *The Enthusiasm of Desmond O'Malley*

The Affair of the Sherlock Holmes Manuscript, as Sheridan Haynes afterwards thought of it, began with a call from Desmond O'Malley, his agent. Desmond's voice was, as always, enthusiastic, and as always seemed hardly containable within an ordinary telephone receiver, more suited to addressing a public meeting.

'Tremendous news, Sher,' he said. For Desmond all news conveyed by telephone was good, tremendous or superlative. Bad news he sent by letter. But still, Sheridan Haynes reflected, optimism is a virtue in an agent. 'Hold on to your hat.' Sher resisted a temptation to say he never wore a hat indoors, and waited for the next words, which came reverently but still forcefully down the line. 'Warren Waymark.'

'The American tycoon?'

'*Tycoon*.' Desmond was indignant at such an understatement. 'A legend in his lifetime. A recluse. The second or third richest man in the world. A man who has cut himself off from all public life, yet—'

'Desmond, I have heard of Warren Waymark. I may even have read the magazine article from which you are quoting. What has he to do with me?'

Desmond's voice took on a creamy, wheedling tone. 'He is the greatest living expert on Sherlock Holmes.'

'That's certainly not true. He is a collector of books and manuscripts about Sherlock Holmes, which is a different thing. Please, Desmond, come to the point.'

'He wants you to put on a special performance of your Holmes readings, just for him. Alone. In person.'

'Is that all?'

'*All?* Do you know what he's offered?' And Desmond mentioned what was certainly a large sum of money. 'Think of the publicity spin-off. I'll be frank with you, Sher, things haven't been easy lately as you know as well as me, this may mean happy days are here again.'

'I don't know about this, Desmond.'

'You don't *know*,' Desmond echoed unbelievingly.

'I'm not sure I want to go on. With the readings, I mean.'

'*Not go on.*' Desmond's voice blended disbelief, horror and dismay, then became that of an adult speaking soothingly to a fractious child. After a couple of minutes Sher said he would think about it and call back.

The readings had come about through the publicity attendant on Sher's solution of what the press called the Karate Killings, at a time when he was playing Sherlock Holmes in a TV series.* An American lecture agency had engaged him to give a series of readings from the Holmes stories, acting the various parts as Emlyn Williams did with Dickens. They had begun with the States, gone on to Australia and Canada, and then Desmond had taken over from the American agency and had arranged a British tour. But the readings imposed an emotional and physical strain, Sher's wife Val had got tired of following him around and settled down to decorating and furnishing their newly-bought small house in Fulham, and he had also begun to feel that he might suffer the fate of being typecast that can come to any actor firmly identified in the

*See *A Three Pipe Problem.*

public mind with a particular role. Desmond merely smiled when he suggested working in a straight play or on TV, and said Sherlock had made him a national name. Indeed, Desmond had made a booking for his next appearance, which was to be in Copenhagen.

He talked to Val. She was looking at an auction catalogue, frowning a little as she marked off items. She had sold the lease of her antique shop in Greenwich and set up in the Fulham Road, no more than five minutes' walk from where they lived. The stock was similar but the prices were higher, and she did very well or so it seemed to Sher, although Val said she ran the shop to avoid getting bored. She showed more interest in the Waymark reading than he had expected.

'I thought you were in favour of my giving them up.'

'Perhaps, but haven't I always said there's nobody I'd sooner live with than Sherlock Holmes? Lucky I feel that way, isn't it.' She waved a hand at the Holmesiana around the living room, the wall covered with photographs of every actor who had played Sherlock Holmes, from William Gillette to John Wood and Sher himself, the row of Toby jugs in the shapes of Holmes, Watson, Moriarty and Mycroft. 'What I said was that if you were going to play some other parts Desmond had better look out for them before you start drawing the old age pension.' Her smile took the sting from the words. Sher was what he sometimes called a very old-fashioned forty-eight, Val ten years younger. 'But to get inside Warren Waymark's fortress, that would be something. Would you really be doing the show to an audience of one?'

'I'm not sure. I don't even know if there's a stage. I think I shall just say no.'

'It's a lot of money. And I'd love to go down there. You don't seem to understand about Waymark. He lives in this castle he built, never goes out, lots of guards around, some people even think he's dead. Why don't you say you can't decide till you've had a look in person, seen if it's suitable?

I mean, perhaps the acoustics are hopeless or something like that.'

'I could just say no.'

'Where's your spirit of adventure? Sherlock never said no.'

When he went to see Desmond and told him this, however, the agent put both pudgy hands flat on his leather-topped desk. 'A visit of inspection? Sher, that's just not possible.'

'All right then, call it off.'

'If that's what you want. If you can afford to throw away money. I can't myself, but I'm only the man who wears his fingers to the bone getting you work. You're free to say no, of course you are.' Desmond's rubbery features were not suited to any expression but that of professional cheerfulness, but he did his best to look both wounded and reproachful.

'Where did the enquiry come from?'

'You've heard of the Prime Minister?'

'Of course, but what has the Prime Minister got to do with it?'

'Ah Sher, you sweet old thing, you shouldn't be allowed out.' Tears filled Desmond's eyes, he used a silk handkerchief to wipe them away. 'The Prime Minister I mean is Paul Decker, they call him Waymark's Prime Minister, he's supposed to handle every single detail of the Mogul's life. That's what they call Waymark, the Mogul.'

'All this must come from the most vulgar elements of the media, papers I never see.'

'Except when they call you the great detective who solved the Karate Killings,' Desmond said cheerfully. 'But it's not just those vulgar elements who've run features about the Mogul and his Prime Minister, reporters from the class papers have managed to get into Castle Baskerville, although they've soon found themselves out on their necks. You *must* know about that.'

'I know of Waymark as a collector of anything to do with Sherlock Holmes, and I've heard he lives in seclusion at a place he has renamed Castle Baskerville. Why should I have known anything more? I take it you had a communication from this man Decker.'

'Not the PM himself, his secretary. He said the Mogul had read about you with the greatest interest, and would be honoured—' Desmond lingered on the word, rolled his eyes slightly, '—if you could find time to give a private and personal reading for him.'

'Did you ask whether there were proper stage facilities?'

'My dear old Sher, this is a one man reading, your only prop is a lectern— '

'Quite true. Nevertheless it is also true that I perform on a stage, that some sound effects are used, and that there is a distance between the performer and his audience. True further that I have never performed before an audience of one. Would it be just one person, or would Mr Decker be present, and perhaps other invited guests? Are the acoustics reasonable? Those are things I should like to know before committing myself.'

'Sher, Sher, I don't understand you. Shall I try to up the ante, is that what you're after?'

'I've told you what I want, to inspect the conditions under which I shall be working. That seems to me perfectly reasonable, given the unusual nature of the occasion.'

'The way you say it. You should have been acting with Frank Benson, or maybe that's too modern, maybe I mean with Irving.'

Sher bent what he knew to be the effective Holmesian hawklike gaze on his agent. 'I take that as a compliment, Desmond. I ought to add that I should like Val to be with me. I am giving a reading in Copenhagen, as you know. Assuming an inspection is satisfactory, I am free after I return.'

'An inspection, they'll never agree.'

'Then I shall be happy to forget the suggestion.'

'The things I do for clients.'

The following telephone call seemed to consist of Desmond saying *yes* and *no*, and beginning phrases cut off by the voice at the other end, phrases like 'I can assure you that—' and 'Of course it won't be necessary to—' and 'Mr Haynes merely wishes to be sure of—'. After cradling the telephone he wiped his face with the silk handkerchief. 'That was the man himself.'

'Waymark?'

'The Prime Minister. Even on the phone you could tell he's somebody special. Decisive. Brisk. But polite with it. What a man.'

'I take it the answer is yes, since you ended by saying that on behalf of Mr Haynes you were sincerely grateful.'

'The answer is yes.'

2 Castle Baskerville

In the forty-eight hours before they visited Castle Baskerville Sher learned more about the Mogul and his entourage. Or rather Val did, by talking to a friend who ran a newspaper cuttings library (she had friends everywhere), which produced a mass of photocopied material. She read it eagerly, sitting with legs tucked under her in an armchair, smoking, and making notes. As Sher drove down to Devon she told him what she had pieced together from the various semi-factual and speculative stories.

Sher was at the wheel of their BMW less from his enjoyment of driving than because of the emotional traumas he experienced as a passenger with Val. She was a skilful but impetuous driver, always confident that she could pass through the gap between two lorries, weaving in and out of traffic, impatient with those who did not get out of the way when she wanted to pass them in the fast lane. He felt little hammers beating in his head at the end of a long journey made as passenger when Val was driving. It was possible, he reflected, that she felt much the same way about being driven by him. She made no comment on his driving but chain-smoked, sometimes closing her eyes with the cigarette in her mouth, so that she might have seemed unconscious but for the jets coming from her nostrils. On this occasion, however, she talked and smoked, waving the cigarette. Sher kept his eyes on the road and listened.

Waymark was in his late sixties, or by some accounts his early seventies. He had been born in the American Northwest, almost certainly in Montana, the fifth child of Abel 'The Tongue' Ekman, a Swedish immigrant to the United States who was given his nickname because of his fluency as stump preacher and medicine salesman. Warren's mother was one of several women who drifted in and out of the Tongue's life. She had parted company with Ekman when the child was two or three years old, and died soon afterwards. Warren travelled round with his father until he was ten, and was then consigned to the care of Ekman's brother Nils, a Lutheran whose life was as strict and orderly as Abel's had been raffish and haphazard. Nils had a clothing shop in a small Illinois town. He sent Warren to school, something unknown to him during life with Abel. There he was jeered at for his ignorance, ran away, was brought back and beaten, and when he was fourteen ran away again, this time for good. He got a job with a shop that sold men's clothing in another small Illinois town, telling William Telford who owned it that he had worked in the business since the age of eight, when he was put into it by his father, a tailor. At the same time he changed his name to Waymark, legend said because this was the name of the district where the shop was situated.

From that time on his life was a success story. Within a couple of years he was buying clothes for Telford, going with him to Chicago to deal with the wholesalers. By the time he was nineteen he had arranged with one wholesaler that he should be set up in his own business, the backer getting a cut of the profits. At twenty-one he had half a dozen shops. He then jettisoned his backer and made another deal with a clothing manufacturer by which he was able to market his famous Waymark to Wearer scheme.

'After that it was upwards, upwards all the way, with occasional problems solved by a bit of villainy.'

'What sort of villainy?'

'Trouble with the Garment Workers' Union, lots of it. Picketing of his manufacturers, blacking their sales to other companies and so on. Waymark seems to have called on the Mafia for help, and presumably made some sort of pact with them, though nothing was ever firmly established. Rumour is the Mafia took a large percentage of the profits from our hero's various activities. After World War II these diversified, as they say, partly into selling arms, about which he seems to have operated with fine impartiality, acting as middle man in deals with the Israelis, Syria, PLO, two or three African states. Mind you, none of this has ever been absolutely proved, he's used so many agents that even tough researchers only say things like "There appear to be significant links between" and "It looks reasonable that". He also made a lot of money in the market, went into electronics at the right time, formed a film company after the war and backed some films that made the cash register ring, got out at the right time too, just before the TV age began. Moved into the soft porn market, took the precaution of buying up a lot of distributors so that his mags got the best displays and rivals were unaccountably sold out or copies were late. Got out of that too when a crackdown was rumoured. He had a magic touch, our hero.'

'You say *had*.'

'That's right. Quite a bit of this is ancient history.' Val stubbed out a cigarette, lighted another. 'In 1970 he was admitted to hospital with some unknown disease. The hospital was— ' she riffled through the sheets of photocopies, ' —the Warren Waymark Hospital in Butte, Montana, built and endowed by him, accordingly and not surprisingly prepared to do anything he asked. He was rumoured to be suffering from some kind of leukaemia. He was in hospital for three months, then emerged said to be much better. There are photographs that show him leaving hospital in a wheelchair, so muffled up it's impossible to tell whether he was the man who went in. Rumours that he died in hospital have been strengthened by the fact that he's never appeared in public since he came out. Mind you, he was never keen on the limelight, even when he had his film flutter he never visited Hollywood. In 1971 he bought a place on Dartmoor called Greatifex Grange, had it knocked down and rebuilt, and renamed it Castle Baskerville. And there he is. Or of course isn't.'

'Do you mean nobody's managed to take a picture of him since 1970?'

'No, I don't mean to say that. But I can't show you the pix, can I, because you daren't take your eyes off the road. What about stopping for lunch?'

'We were going to call on Brinsley.'

'At your speed we wouldn't be there for dinner.'

Brinsley, Sher's elder brother, lived just outside Okehampton. He was a doctor in general practice, who irritated Val by the air of condescension with which he treated Sher's theatrical and detectival activities.

'Perhaps we can see him on the way back,' Sher agreed.

They ate at a pub between Honiton and Exeter that said 'Pub Grub' outside, but provided only ham sandwiches and doubtfully fresh pies within. There Val showed him before and after hospital photographs of Waymark. There were several pictures from the early period, showing a lean, hungry-looking young man with a long narrow head. From the Fifties and early Sixties there were more which showed him leaner and narrower, these aspects emphasised by one revealing him in swimming trunks, lean-shanked and almost emaciated, beside a plump blonde. Another blonde, very similar but fully dressed, was seen in another picture. In a third Waymark was outside a restaurant with a man who stood with arms folded, smiling confidently at the camera. The caption said: 'Tycoon Warren Waymark and chief aide Gene Van Helder.'

The wheelchair photograph, as Val had said, could have

been anybody. Three later ones, all taken surreptitiously by visitors to Castle Baskerville, were not much more informative. One showed a man who could have been Waymark walking in the Castle grounds, hands behind his back. In another he was at the dining table with a glass at his mouth partly concealing his face, and the third showed a head and shoulders that might, allowing for the passage of time, have been that of the man in the early photographs. In all these later pictures, even the one at the dining table, he wore dark glasses.

Sher put them down and steepled his fingers, a Holmesian habit that had become natural to him after long practice in the TV series. 'There is a particular reason for thinking this is the real Warren Waymark.' He paused, but Val only looked at him, denying him a Watsonic reply. 'The fact that he wants to commission a performance of my readings.'

'It's a point. But why is he never seen in public, why won't he be photographed, why does he live in a sort of fortress? I'd have thought those questions might have stirred your detective instincts. Let me tell you something else. You saw that picture of Waymark with Van Helder. Before Waymark went into hospital Van Helder was absolutely the man you approached if you wanted anything – to see Waymark, put a business proposition, anything at all. Decker was there but in a subsidiary position, just one of the sidekicks Waymark kept around, playing them off against each other, making one the flavour of the month, as it were.'

'You mean Waymark's homosexual?'

She laughed. 'Oh no, not gay, just mischievous. Has a weakness for buxom blondes as shown, married two of them though neither lasted long, both left with handsome settlements. Some time near the end of the Seventies Van Helder left and Decker became Prime Minister. There's an article by a Van Helder man who left at the same time as his boss, and he tells a tale about Decker gradually persuading Waymark that Van Helder had been cheating him for years, and forcing him out. However it happened, Decker replaced Van Helder.

The most recent story, in one of the more sensational of our glorious tabloids, says that a new lady was installed a few months back, the Mogul's feeble but still around, and nothing happens without the PM's approval. This reporter got in by some unstated means, probably bribing one of the staff, was found out, roughed up, slung out, camera smashed. The PM is no softie. Don't you think it's fascinating? I wouldn't have missed it for worlds.'

'I think it's none of our business. And that, even though we're not looking in on Brinsley, we ought to get on.'

She made a face at him. 'Pompous sod.'

An involuntary shudder passed through Sheridan Haynes, shaking his body so that his hand trembled on the wheel, and Val called out in alarm to ask what was the matter.

'That stretch of green, so bright it looks unreal. I thought of the account of the great Grimpen Mire in the *Hound* – you remember? – where a false step meant death to man or beast, and Watson heard the dreadful cry of the pony sucked down in the quagmire. I thought for a moment that I felt the presence of evil, or something like it. You'll think I'm old-fashioned, sentimental.'

He stopped the car. Rain lashed down with force that obscured the windscreen, pattered on the roof with a sound like that of small running feet. Val put her hand over his until he ceased to tremble, then said they could give up the whole thing and go to see Brinsley if he wished. He shook his head. They drove on over the moor, and fifteen minutes later got their first glimpse of Castle Baskerville. As they did so the sun came out, so that they saw the place with a rainbow stretching over it. Within the radiant semi-circle of the rainbow the Castle looked unreal, castellated walls, central tower and drawbridge giving it the air of a child's plaything. Around it stretched the moor, lushly green, with no other house in sight. Sher shook his head in disbelief.

'It looks like something out of Disneyland,' Val said. 'And

so it is. I'll bet you'd find its counterpart in California. That's just about the limit of our hero's imagination.'

The rain stopped, the rainbow faded. They reached wire fencing and a gate. A sign on the gate said: 'Private. Visitors Not Welcome. Fence and Gate Electrified. Do Not Touch. Guard Dogs Roam Freely. If Information needed use Telephone by Gate.'

'And welcome to Castle Baskerville,' Val said.

Sher got out of the car, went to the telephone which was on a post beside the gate, lifted the receiver. A man's voice said, 'Guard house. State your business.'

'To see Mr Waymark.'

'Name?'

Sher prided himself on his Holmesian calm, but found it deserting him. 'My name is Sheridan Haynes. I am accompanied by my wife, and we are here at Mr Waymark's request. I consider this reception grossly discourteous. If the gate is not opened immediately I shall leave.'

The rasping voice said, 'Coming down.'

Half a minute later a small van appeared, and a man jumped out of it. He wore a greenish grey tunic, and trousers that looked like a cross between Army fatigues and Chinese peasant clothes. The military impression was strengthened by a shoulder flash that read *Guard*. A whistle hung from his neck. He stood on the other side of the white-painted gate and said, 'Credentials.'

'This is preposterous.'

The guard spoke slowly and clearly, like somebody recording or repeating a message. 'Mister, you told me your name, but how do I know it's right? You got to prove it. Driving licence, letters to you, whatever you got.'

'Your requests are ludicrous.' Sher could not resist ticking off points on fingers. 'One, you appear to be in no doubt that Sheridan Haynes has an appointment with Mr Waymark. Two, you ask for proof of my identity. But three, does it not occur to you that if I were an impostor I should certainly have provided myself with such proofs in order to deceive you? Let me make it clear that I refuse—'

'Sher.' Val was out of the car and standing beside him. 'Do it.'

'Do what?'

'Show him your driving licence.'

The guard looked at the licence, took from his pocket a dingus with buttons on it, pressed one of the buttons. The gate opened. They followed the van. The road rose gently, and at the top they had another view of the Castle, now perhaps fifty yards away. This close it looked no less like something in a child's game. The water in the moat surrounding it was still as glass, the drawbridge was drawn up, the portcullis down. They drove to the edge of the moat. The guard got out of the van, aimed the dingus at some part of the portcullis. It rose slowly and the drawbridge came down. They crossed it, and stopped just inside, beside what looked like a small grey brick lodge.

A man came out of this lodge. He wore a version of the guard's clothing, plus a burnished brown belt with a pistol holster, and a peaked green and grey cap which was slightly at an angle. His shoulder flash said *Gate Officer*. He lifted a hand to the cap, almost touching it, opened Val's car door, stood beside it to hand her out.

'Welcome to Castle Baskerville.'

They were in a large courtyard. Behind them were the outer walls, ahead the bulk of the Castle which could now be seen to consist of a dominating central block with large wings on either side which had been extended at the ends to make a rough E shape. Access to the whole was given through a wide archway over which had been carved in Gothic lettering, 'Castle Baskerville, 1972'.

'Remarkable, isn't it? Mr Waymark had it done to his own design. He wanted a combination of a castle and a country house.'

The Gate Officer was jaunty, he had a reassuring air of

regarding the Castle and his duties there as rather a lark. Within the lodge he took off the peaked cap and revealed springing curly hair, youthfully rosy cheeks. They were in a room that seemed to combine the qualities of living room, office and military guardroom. It was in two parts, divided by a counter that stretched across the width of the room. On one side of this counter were easy chairs and a TV set, on the other two desks, a row of filing cabinets. A door at the far end said 'Armoury', and beside it was another which read 'Inspection Room'. On the wall were printed notices: 'Visitors *must* report to Guard House on arrival and departure', 'Visitors *must* be inspected', 'No unauthorised person to enter Armoury', and 'Check it First with Mr Hurst'.

The Gate Officer lifted a flap and moved to the other side of the counter, still smiling. Val sat in one of the easy chairs and lighted a cigarette. Sher said, 'I can't say we've been made to feel welcome.'

'I'm sorry. We have to go by the book even with a distinguished visitor, and I'd slipped out for a minute. But at least in your case we can waive inspection.'

'Very good of you. What is inspection?'

'A body check. Not primarily for arms, though nobody carrying a firearm is admitted.' When Sher asked why anybody should want to come in with a firearm the young man smiled at him. 'Just a precaution. Cameras are the thing. Only last week a journalist tried to get in saying he was from the Sewage Department, wanted to inspect the drains. Had a neat little camera zipped into an inside pocket, micro recorder in his lapel. So we have to be careful. But you and Mrs Haynes, that's different. I'll just call through to say you're here. By the way, I'm Brian.'

Val said, 'Are you going to check us first with Mr Hurst, Brian?'

He laughed, showing neat white teeth, then turned to the switchboard and spoke in a voice too low to be audible. He turned back to them smiling again, a dimple in his cheek.

'If you leave the car keys I'll see your BMW is put under cover and brought round when you leave. Mr Waymark looks forward to seeing you. Eric will take you over. I'm afraid no smoking is permitted in the Castle, it affects Mr Waymark's breathing.'

Val stubbed out her cigarette. 'Satisfy my curiosity about one thing. Do you carry anything in that holster?'

'Why, yes.' The young man turned away, then whirled round as in a cowboy film, slightly crouched, blue pistol in hand. He twirled it, held it out. 'Colt .38, police special. Never had an occasion to use it in my time here.'

Eric, the incongruously named guard, preceded them across the courtyard. They passed beneath the arch, turned left and confronted a large oak door with a brass knocker in the shape of a dog's head. Eric knocked, and the door was opened by a maid in cap and apron, who sketched a curtsey.

They were in a large high hall, with great timber rafters stretching up into the roof. Around the walls were stags' heads between the stained glass windows that showed knights jousting, kneeling to kiss the hands of their mistresses, and hunting followed by hounds. The windows made the light dim even on this now sunny September day. In an enormous fireplace large logs burned. At one end of the hall was a double staircase with above it a large balustraded gallery.

Something about this staircase and gallery, or perhaps about the windows, stirred an unidentifiable memory in Sher's mind. Val stretched a hand to the logs and whispered: 'Electric.'

A man appeared out of the shadows at the top of the double staircase, came down it slowly. As he entered the area of light provided by faintly hissing gas mantles in the hall he was revealed as slight, with sandy complexion and neat, pinched features. Above a narrow nose pale eyes peered at them over gold-rimmed half-moon spectacles. He wore a blue suit with a faint pinstripe, a white shirt, a plain blue tie. His lips were bloodless lines, his voice subdued.

'Mr and Mrs Haynes. Please come with me.'

He led the way back to the staircase. Sher said, 'You're taking us to Mr Waymark,' making the words a statement rather than an interrogation.

'Mr Decker said he would like to see you when you arrived.' They reached the gallery. A corridor ran off it to left and right. They turned left, went through a door covered in green baize, and entered surroundings so different that the effect was almost shocking.

The aquarium gloom of the hall below was replaced here by strip lighting, the Eastern rugs in the hall by modern carpet. The sounds of typewriters, voices, a ticker tape machine, could be heard from the rooms leading off the corridor down which they walked. Their guide said, 'Those are the offices. The Mogul still has an interest in various international enterprises.'

'Which you handle for him? Or does he deal with business affairs himself?'

The question came from Val. Their guide stopped as though considering it, but Sher saw that he had pressed a barely visible button in the wall. 'You might say I am the administrator of Castle Baskerville.'

'Mr Hurst?' He looked at Val over the tiny glasses, then agreed that was his name. 'Check it first with Mr Hurst. I hope everyone does.'

He considered the remark seriously. 'I handle matters of detail, that is true.' In front of them a lift door opened. They got in.

'But Mr Waymark makes the decisions,' Val said. 'Or the Prime Minister?'

Hurst did not reply. They went up one floor, got out, entered a large comfortable living room where a man sat on a sofa reading the *Financial Times*. He jumped up and came towards them, hand outstretched.

'Mr and Mrs Haynes, very good of you to come. I'm Paul Decker. Many thanks, Gordon, for bringing them up in person. Gordon runs the whole damn place,' he said confidingly. Hurst said it had been a pleasure, left.

Paul Decker was a stocky man with a large head. His features were well shaped and powerful, his body perhaps bulkier than it should have been. He wore a casual dark blue cashmere jacket, paler blue trousers tightly belted, brown reverse calf shoes. A scar on his right cheek gave him an air of toughness. His grey eyes were watchful, but he laughed readily, as he did now when he offered a cigarette and Val hesitated.

'You've been told not to smoke? That's so when you're with the Mogul, but we're off limits here. I can't tell you how glad I am you're prepared to consider the idea. He's been talking about nothing else for days.'

'Shall we be able to see Mr Waymark? I've read that he's an invalid.'

'He has his bad days, but nothing would stop him from seeing you. I wanted to have a word first, that's all. I don't know if you've read the press stories? No, that's stupid, Sheridan Haynes wouldn't come here without being clued up. I just want you to know most of them are crap. They're not exactly all lies, it's just that these media boys find a few pea-size nuggets and pretend they're gold bricks. Take the move to this place. The Mogul's been sold on England for years, says it's the only civilised country in Europe, everything runs nice and slow. And you know what he feels about Sherlock Holmes. So why be surprised when he comes to live here, builds himself a place and calls it by a name out of the Sherlock stories? Which I have to tell you always seemed pretty old-fashioned to me. You'll take a dish of tea? You see I've learned a few local phrases over the years.'

A young man entered the room, bearing a tray with teapot and cups, scones and jam. He too was stocky, snub-nosed, wavy haired. He wore jeans, and a white shirt frilled at cuffs and neck. 'This is Jimmy. He can pour tea without spilling it and hand plates round without leaving a thumbmark on them. He can also look after himself and me too, if it should be necessary. Jimmy, meet Sheridan Haynes the famous actor, and Mrs Haynes.'

'Pleased to meet you,' Jimmy said, without sounding as if that was the case. The teacups and plates were Minton, the jam came in a silver pot. Decker waited until Jimmy was out of the room before speaking again.

'You may like to know something about the set-up here. When this place was rebuilt it was done exactly the way the Mogul wanted. He's a recluse, that's one thing the news stories have got right, and it's true his health isn't good. Doc Prettyman lives here, and is on call if the Mogul wants him, also looks after the staff. And there's a nurse. How ill is the Mogul? Hard to know, Dave Prettyman says it's partly hypochondria, he's no more sick than I am. I have a mild case of diabetes, which is why I'm not eating the scones and jam, as I see you've noticed.'

'The scones are delicious,' Val said. Decker nodded, smiled.

'What else should I tell you? The Mogul says he's got the biggest collection of Holmes films in the world, and I believe him. I see him most days for an hour or so, to go over business details. We've cut down a lot since we came here, mostly on the advice of our lawyer George Darnley. There are things the Mogul should never have gotten into, but Waymark Enterprises is still an international business, mostly concerned these days with food and clothing. I make the day-to-day decisions, but they all get the man's okay. Apart from seeing me, Doc Prettyman and Lavender who looks after him, he's pretty much a hermit. That's the way he wants it.'

Val said, 'No feminine companionship?'

Decker laughed. 'You have a point. Why yes, some feminine companionship, though maybe not what you think. He likes to talk about the past and has what he calls his listeners, who are always women. Maybe other things happen, I don't know, he's a hermit not a monk. But the rest of us, people who live here, we're not hermits. Hence there are two wings in the Castle, this one where I have a suite and the business side of the operation goes on, and another which houses the Mogul and his nurse Lavender, plus cinema. Then there are the residential and entertainment complexes in the grounds, away from the house – Castle, rather. That's where the people who work here live, clerks, cooks and bottlewashers, et cetera.'

'Cooks, bottlewashers and guards,' Sher said.

Decker leaned forward, spoke earnestly. 'Try to understand. It's an unusual society here, of course I know that. Shut up a lot of people in an enclosure, then tell them they're free and at the same time put all sorts of restrictions on them, and you get lots of friction. Jealousy, envy, petty squabbles, and sometimes it isn't so petty.'

'Do you mean you need guards for them?'

'Not exactly. The Mogul doesn't want to see people, and I'm here to see he doesn't, and to see nobody plays tricks on him. Not long ago there was a man who claimed to have prints of some early silents, Holmes stuff that had never been shown, with a man I'd never heard of playing Sherlock.'

'Eille Norwood?'

'Sounds right. This man said they were unique, couldn't trust the post, must show them to Mr Waymark in person. Turned out they were fakes, bits of old film spliced together. The Mogul spotted they were fakes in five minutes, had the man thrown out. He was upset though, said we should have been more careful.'

'Isn't it a job to get people to stay?' Val asked. 'Don't they get sick of it?'

'Right you are. The pay's good. They get eight weeks' holiday a year, there's an indoor swimming pool, gymnasium, tennis courts, cinema. But yes, there are problems. Except for weekends off and holidays you stay in the grounds, no visits to local pubs, had to put a stop to that, staff blabbed to journalists after they'd had a few pints. That's mostly what the guards are for, to make sure people don't get out when they shouldn't, as well as getting in. Gordon does the hiring and firing, and if you look at how thin the stuff is that gets through to the press you'll see he does it pretty well.' He looked from one to the other of them, gave his easy laugh.

'You're wondering why I'm telling you all this? Just to prepare you for meeting the man. Believe me, preparation is needed. Did I say anything about light? The Mogul believes he suffers from photophobia, inability to bear strong light. He's been examined by specialists and they can't find much physically wrong, but then photophobia's a nervous condition except in albinos, so who's to say he hasn't got it? You'll find the lighting dim. Then he's got a mild form of eczema that affects his hands and thinks diseases are passed by touch, so don't expect him to shake hands, not even though he's wearing gloves. I hope you didn't put off any other engagement to come here.'

'On Tuesday Sher's going to Copenhagen to give his Sherlock Holmes reading, so you might call this a holiday before he goes,' Val said. 'Then the following week's free.'

'You mean you might come down here then? That would be wonderful. But forgive me, you'll want to meet the Mogul first, and look at the facilities for the reading.' He spoke into a wall telephone, turned back to them. 'Lavender says everything's okay, he'll see us now. Why hallo, Dave, come and meet our distinguished visitors. Mr and Mrs Sheridan Haynes, this is Dave Prettyman, our resident medic.'

'Good to know you. Hope I'm not butting in on anything important.' Doctor Prettyman was tall and thin, with a lantern jaw and a powerful growth of five o'clock shadow. He had small deepset eyes that looked from one to the other of them uneasily, as if he knew they were unlikely to believe anything he said, although in fact it amounted to no more than that he had seen the Mogul that morning, and he was perfectly fine.

'Paul, I wanted to tell you I gotta take a few days' leave. Going off today, be back next Thursday. I checked this out with Gordon, he said okay if it's all right with you.'

'So long as the Mogul's in good shape you have my blessing. Enjoy yourself, Dave.' The doctor looked doubtful about that, but managed a smile. When he had gone Decker elaborated. 'I told you living here was a strain. Dave's a good doctor, the Mogul trusts him and does what he says, but every so often he just has to cut loose. You might not think it, but Dave's a poker player, got himself in bad trouble back home when he was up to his neck or a bit higher in debts to some pretty rough characters. My guess would be that he's going off looking for some action. He leaves a number with Gordon Hurst in case we need him urgently, but that's never happened. Let's go.'

They returned the way they had come, but when they reached the double staircase went straight ahead instead of going back to the hall. 'Lavender's the nurse. Fairly new, Gordon hired him a few months back, and Dave gave his okay. The nurse before him had kind of a nervous breakdown. Can't say I'm surprised, being next door to the Mogul several hours a day isn't the most cheerful way of spending your time, but Lavender's coped. So far.'

The lighting in this part of the Castle was by electric lamps of very low wattage. Decker tapped on a door, and it was opened by a tall man who stood aside to let them into a room in which the windows were of darkened glass. The effect was a kind of twilight, in which chairs and tables were dimly visible. They were discernibly ancient, or at least Victorian rather than modern.

'I'm Lavender,' the tall man said. 'This way. Take care now.' He put a guiding hand on Val's arm, and as they passed near one of the lamps she saw with slight surprise that Lavender was black. He opened another door and stood aside.

This room had the same twilight effect except for a bright square patch on one wall. There was a click, the patch disappeared. A man got up from an armchair and said, 'A pleasure and honour to meet the most truthful representation of the great detective.' He moved past Val and came close to Sher, who automatically put out a hand. 'You must excuse me. Unfortunately I suffer from a skin disease, a rare variety of eczema which is worsened by any kind of contact with another skin. I am wearing gloves but still I cannot risk it, Mr Haynes, I cannot risk it.' His voice was dry, thin and crisp. Chairs had been placed in a rough semi-circle round Waymark's own armchair, in which he sat down again gingerly. Lavender hovered a moment, then retreated.

'I apologise also for the near darkness in which I have to live. Perhaps Paul has told you of my extreme sensitiveness to light. If I drew the curtains, within a few minutes I should be in bed with a severe migraine, lightning flashes before my eyes, a feeling that my eyeballs were being screwed round and round.'

'But you can watch television,' Sher said.

Waymark gave a choked laugh. 'I can, yes, but only if I wear these.' He held up a pair of spectacles placed on the arm of his chair. 'They are made from a special plastic which reduces the light rays that are so agonisingly painful. Wearing them I can watch television, even walk briefly in the grounds without suffering the lightning flashes that make my life a misery. Unhappily it doesn't last. After a little while in daylight I am driven indoors. I can watch the magic box for two or three hours, but then the shooting pains come and signal to me that it is time to stop.' He put on the glasses. 'I have been watching for only a few minutes, there is no reason why I should compel you to sit in the dark. Paul, will you be good enough to draw the curtains.'

Decker walked across, pulled the curtain cord. The windows here were also of darkened glass, but an oak panelled room was revealed, with bookcases lining two walls, a fireplace similar to that in the hall below but smaller, and worn, blackened rafters. Beyond the windows was an expanse of lawn. But it was at their host that Sher and Val looked. The glasses, large and almost black, hid the eyes, but the man in the armchair might certainly have been the one in the photographs. The face, very thin, narrow, deeply lined, was topped by untidy strands of silver-grey hair. The gloves went almost up to the wrist. He wore a long black dressing gown and red slippers and when he got up, as he did now, beside the bulk of Decker he seemed insubstantial, a ghost rather than a man. And yet, Sher thought, if we could see his eyes this impression might be changed. He did not believe that eyes were the windows of the soul, but still a face without eyes was a kind of blank, one did not know what went on behind it.

Waymark turned the black glasses on to Sher, spoke to him as if they were alone. 'To be an exile from the world of nature is not a happy fate, Mr Haynes. It means one is less than half alive. The brain remains alert, but what interest can an invalid have in what goes on in the world? I have put such things aside, as I have put aside the pleasures of the table. About that too I had no choice, for my digestion is ruined. The magic screen and the greatest detective of fiction, those are my consolations. What was your impression of the great hall below?'

'It seemed vaguely familiar. As if I had been there before.'

Again the choked laugh. 'Very good. You have indeed been there, although it was not reproduced in quite such faithful detail. You recall *The Hound of the Baskervilles*, and the hall Watson entered with Sir Henry Baskerville.'

Sher put a hand to his head, one of the Holmesian gestures that had become second nature. 'Of course. The stained glass windows, the panelling, the stags' heads – and the gallery round the top of the hall. They are all in the story.'

'Just so. I left out the coats of arms on the walls – I just don't qualify for them. I'm delighted with you, Mr Haynes. Let me show you some of the things I have here that I'm sure will interest you. All the first editions of the books, of course, and the *Beeton's Christmas Annual* appearance of *A Study in Scarlet*, but one or two other things are—' He chuckled, left the sentence unfinished.

Val joined Decker where he stood looking out through the darkened French windows. He opened them, they went down steps to a lawn. She asked if Waymark ever came out here. 'I seem to have seen a photograph of him outside.'

'You can't take everything he says as gospel. He may not take any interest in politics, but I can tell you he doesn't sign any piece of paper without finding out what it commits him to, though he leaves the detailed stuff to me. And if he really wants to look at things he can do it, so the doctors say. Mind you, I don't doubt he *thinks* he's got agonising pains, but it's wonderful how they disappear when he's doing something like showing your husband his Sherlock stuff. And I don't believe he's lost interest in the ladies either.'

'But if he can't bear to be touched—' She looked at him. They both began to laugh.

'Mrs Haynes, I can see we've got the same sense of humour. The Mogul and his ladies is one of the mysteries of Castle Baskerville that I've never tried to solve. Maybe he does just talk to them, maybe it's all part of the game of let's pretend he plays with the world.'

They walked across the lawn and looked back. To one side stood the bulk of the Castle, to the other two long blocks of buildings that might have been part of a modern university.

'Over there the bedrooms, swimming pool, dining hall and so on,' Decker said. 'The whole thing is what you English call a folly, isn't it?'

'It's not a folly, it's a monster. I don't know how you were ever allowed to build it.'

'You know what they say, everything's possible if you have enough money. And what harm does it do to anyone, no neighbours to be upset, and the ponies have never objected. Ah, here comes the listener in residence.'

A woman came towards them from one of the modern blocks. Her long fair hair was shoulder length, her face had an ordinary prettiness. Plucked arched eyebrows over large blue eyes gave her a look of perpetual surprise.

'This is Polly Flinders, which isn't her name but it's the one the Mogul has given her. Polly, I expect you knew Mr Haynes the actor was coming today. This is his wife Val.'

'Hi.' Polly put out a small plump hand to be shaken, 'Don't see many strangers. Welcome to the prison house.'

'I don't care for remarks like that,' Decker said gently.

'You got barbed wire all round, guards on the gate, what else would you call it?'

Decker's voice was still gentle. 'You know they're protection for Mr Waymark.'

'Oh, is that all? I'll remember. Enjoy yourself, Mrs Haynes.'

'She could walk out any time she liked, and I shouldn't be sorry,' Decker said. 'Though the Mogul gets fretful without his listener.'

'Mr Decker—'

'Paul.'

'Forgive me for being curious, I *am* curious no use denying it, but how did she come here? I mean, how did she ever get in? Of course if the answer's embarrassing—'

'Val, there are no secrets here, nothing to hide. Polly was a girl friend of Lavender, that's how she got here. He was an actor who never made it and became a male nurse, and she used to work in a strip show which I should say is just about her speed. As I said before it isn't a monastery, some of the staff are married, others have boy friends or girl friends who pay weekend visits. Polly was on a visit, the Mogul happened to glimpse her, bingo. She sees him a couple of hours every day, he says he just talks to her and maybe that's so, though who'd want to talk to Polly Flinders? It seems to keep him happy. The only problem is she and Lavender don't seem to be on the same terms they were, so I'm told, and that makes for friction.'

They found Waymark and Sher seated at a table. Sher cried out, 'Val, come here, this is amazing.' She went over, looked at what seemed to her a rather crude drawing. 'Do you know what this is?'

'Mr Sherlock Holmes, I presume. Though I must say it doesn't look much like him.'

'Look at the inscription.'

She read: 'To Dr Cowan Doyle, in the hope that his Mormon book will lead to others in a similar vein. DHF'.

'Apart from the deduction that whoever wrote it didn't know how to spell Conan—'

Sher said solemnly, 'This is the drawing by D.H. Friston which was the frontispiece for the original appearance of *A Study in Scarlet* in *Beeton's Christmas Annual*. It's the first drawing ever made of Sherlock Holmes. And look at this – Conan Doyle's original manuscript of the play William Gillette used and altered when he first played Holmes on the stage. And the manuscript of *A Study in Scarlet*, some working notes for the *Hound*—' He turned to Waymark. 'Mr Waymark, I owe you an apology. When somebody said you were the greatest Sherlock Holmes collector I expressed doubt. I was wrong.'

'I am glad they please you.' Waymark gave his choked laugh.

'Hey, Warry.' Polly had come in by the French window. 'Listening time.'

The dark glasses were turned on her, the dry voice said, 'Not now, Polly.'

'This is my time to come over.'

'I said not now. Lavender will call when I need you.' She pouted, appeared about to protest further, left them. 'I find therapy, sessions talking in a dark room about anything that comes into my head, are of benefit to the psyche. But I live on my nerves. A man like yourself, Mr Haynes, a great actor, superbly in control of his thoughts, his body, all his movements, has no need of such therapy.' The thin voice crackled, he lowered his head, said almost in a whisper, 'Draw the curtains, I cannot bear the light.' When the day had been shut out he spoke in the same dry whisper. 'It has been a great pleasure to see you. I fear I have become over-excited, I can feel the nerve ends trembling. Forgive me if I ask you to leave now. Paul will show you the theatre, arrange whatever may have to be changed there. But I shall expect you, Mr Haynes, it will be one of the great events of my life to hear your reading. I know you won't fail me.' He did not wait for acknowledgement or reply. 'I am sorry I have to retire.'

As they left the room the white-clad tall figure of Lavender entered by another door.

Decker led the way into a room within the central area of the Castle, and explained that this was Waymark's personal cinema.

'He claims he's got everything ever made about Sherlock on film or TV, and I guess it may be true at that. He's got all your TV films of course, shows them often, says they're the most faithful to the original stories. As you can see, there's a raised area at the end which we hope would serve as a stage. I asked—'

He stopped as the lights went out, and Sher's face appeared on the screen, pipe in mouth, a spiral of smoke rising from it. He wore a dressing gown and sat cross-legged on a mass of pillows and cushions. The titles rolled, saying that these were *The Adventures of Sherlock Holmes* with Sheridan Haynes in 'The Man with the Twisted Lip'. The camera cut to Watson on the other side of the room looking anxiously at Holmes through the haze of smoke. Decker called out, 'That will do,' and said to them, 'I couldn't resist a little demonstration. The Mogul sits in here for hours at a time watching Sherlock movies. He has a control panel so that he can choose any one of a hundred titles.'

The lights went on again, and Jimmy appeared from

the back of the room accompanied by a small black-bearded man. 'This is Bill Hogan,' Decker said. 'Bill, there'd be no problems about any special lighting needed when Mr Haynes comes here to give a reading, would there?' Black beard grunted what might have been assent, staring at Sher intently. Decker accompanied them as they went across to the raised area, and Sher talked about the positioning of the lectern and what he would need in the way of lighting. Hogan's replies seemed almost made at random, and once or twice Decker corrected him sharply. Sher sensed tension in the little man, like that of an actor unsure of his lines. The blackness of the electrician's full set was not matched by his pale eyebrows. When they returned to Val, Decker asked if he was happy with the set.

'The stage is good enough, and there seems nothing wrong with the acoustics, but the lighting won't do. I must be frank, and say I was not impressed by Mr Hogan.'

'Perfectly true he's not an expert. Tell me what you need.'

'It will be necessary for some lighting technicians who worked on the stage production to come down. They know exactly what's needed, and can arrange it in a couple of hours.'

Decker made a note. 'Anything else?'

'Only that I'm not very happy about performing before an audience of one.'

'Okay, okay, I understand. I'll be here, wouldn't miss it, possibly Lavender, maybe Gordon and a couple of others. The Mogul may need a little talking into it, but I'll manage that. We shall all count ourselves privileged. I doubt if Polly's interests extend to Sherlock Holmes, but she might be there too. Now perhaps we can talk about details. If it's a question of money, that isn't important. I'm here to see the Mogul gets what he wants . . .'

Half an hour later they had arranged that Sher would give his performance in two weeks' time. Decker walked with them back to the entrance where their car was waiting, said what a pleasure it had been to talk to Val, left them. When he had gone Brian showed his white teeth, and asked if they had enjoyed themselves.

Val said that wasn't quite the word, Sher did not reply. Through the window of the lodge he had glimpsed for a moment the long blonde hair of Polly Flinders. Then they were away, the outer gate was opened, they were driving across the moor away from Castle Baskerville.

'Something funny,' Val said as she lit her cigarette. 'Something really screwy about the whole set-up. Possibilities noted for Sherlock's attention. It could be an actor playing Waymark, which would explain why nobody gets to see him. Or it could be Waymark's doped to keep him ill, and a prisoner in his own castle. Further thought. We only have Decker's word for it that Waymark looks at papers before he signs them. How does all that strike you?'

'I think you're committing the classic error of theorising without facts.'

'I seem to have heard that one before. Thanks, Sherlock. Any other friendly comments?'

'Waymark certainly wasn't drugged when we saw him. And I don't think there's any doubt we were talking to him, not an actor. He spoke about Sherlock Holmes books and manuscripts, not just the things I showed you, and there's no doubt about his knowledge. I'm sure his collector's passion is genuine.'

'It could have been mugged up to impress you.'

'I don't believe it. He wasn't just reciting a part, he was able to answer questions about the canon he couldn't possibly have foreseen. What I don't understand—'

'So there *is* something you don't understand. Hurrah.'

'Irony does not become you. Why was Hogan wearing a false beard and moustache? Val, do be careful with that cigarette.'

'Are you sure?'

'Yes. His eyebrows were pale, and so was the hair on the

back of his hands. He wore a black full set. Foolish.'

'What a noticing old Sherlock you are. Would you say the game's afoot? Or shall I?'

'No game is afoot. The truth is probably that Waymark is just the eccentric sick man the papers say, and Hogan puts on his full set in the presence of strangers to hide a disfiguring birthmark.'

'You're just a wet blanket.'

'And I do think we ought to call in on Brinsley.'

'Oh, my God.'

They called in, were invited to stay to an excellent meal which Brinsley called a scratch supper, stayed the night and left early in the morning. Brinsley's wife worshipped him in a way Val found infuriating, and Brinsley himself was as affably condescending as ever. She returned to London in a bad temper.

3. Unexpected Meeting with an Old Friend

The visit to Castle Baskerville had been made on a Friday. Sher went to Copenhagen on the following Tuesday. Val had intended to go with him, but in the end he went on his own. One of her best clients, an American lawyer, rang to say he was in England unexpectedly and would like to take her out to lunch, something that had in the past been a prelude to profitable business. At Kastrup Airport there was a reception party of two Danes, plus a little knot of photographers. Sher was escorted to a suite in a hotel at Kongens Nytorv, and agreed to give interviews to *Politiken* and *Berlingske Tidende* on the following morning. Then he was left with Ulrich and Peter, President and Secretary of the Silver Blaze Society of Denmark, which had invited him.

'You know each other, I believe,' Ulrich said.

'I should just about think we do.' Peter was small and round, with a merry clown's face, Ulrich tall and sombre. 'We are old friends.'

'I trust you will make us the honour to attend a small dinner of the Silver Blazers this evening.'

'Unless you have other fish to fry,' Peter said, and winked. His other name was Mortensen, and he was a travel agent who

47

had written Sher a fan letter about his portrayal of the great detective. A few weeks later he had come to London and been Sher's guest at a party given by Moira Wilde, the actress who had played Violet Hunter in 'The Copper Beeches'. At the party Peter's behaviour had been distinctly uninhibited. He had left with a young actress to whom he had been talking, and hinted on the following day that the evening had ended in some kind of orgy which he appeared to think Sher had arranged.

Sher said he would be delighted to attend the dinner.

'Very well. I shall have the pleasure of collecting you at seven o'clock. Now I will leave you if you forgive me.'

'By the way, how is the beautiful Mrs Haynes, Val?' Peter asked archly when they were alone.

'Very well. She runs an antique business and had to stay in London to see an American who'd just flown over.'

'A pity. You love your wife, of course. I too have a charming wife, I love her greatly.' Peter's rubbery mouth turned down momentarily as if he were about to cry. 'But sometimes it is good to be alone in a foreign city, isn't that true? One can go to a party, it is very enjoyable, you remember?'

'The party in London? Yes.'

'The party and after. The little Griselda and her friends, I have not forgotten.'

Sher said, as he had done before, that he had nothing to do with anything that happened after Peter left the party.

'You are discreet. But the elephant never forgets, we shall have a good time here. Girls, girls, I love girls.' Peter snapped his fingers, did a little mock dance, jigging from one foot to another. 'Not tonight, perhaps tomorrow after the reading, eh? Tonight we have a different little surprise for you. Now you will be tired, I leave you to get some rest.'

What kind of surprise? He had an awful vision of some Danish version of a kissogram, perhaps a pudding made in the shape of the Hound of the Baskervilles from which sprang a naked girl who put her arms round his neck, crying 'A kiss from Irene Adler'. But the Danish Sherlockians to whom he was introduced at dinner were grave figures, some bearded, serious students of the master who could not be suspected of consenting to the introduction of naked girls into puddings. Peter stayed beside him, keeping up a running commentary on the other guests, sometimes of a malicious kind.

'Rolfe is a scientific genius, he says so himself. . . Elise is one of our most promising novelists, they said so twenty years ago and are still saying it. . . Anders is a leading light in the Sherlock Holmes Klubben, they are not pleased because it was the Silver Blazers who had the thought of inviting you.' The promised or threatened surprise had passed out of Sher's mind when a figure approached with hand outstretched and Peter said triumphantly, 'Ah *hah*. Here is no need of introduction, I think.'

The red square face, the squat body were unknown to him. Yet there was something. . .

'Hunter's, school dramatic society, we did *Othello*.' The man said to Peter, 'He was an actor even then, belted out the lines like nobody's business. Got carried away too, nearly strangled me one night.' In a ludicrous falsetto he said, ' "Your wife, my lord; your true and loyal wife." '

'Billie Bailey.'

'Bertie, but right you are. It must be, I don't know how many years, twenty or more. We not only knew each other at school, we were up at Oxford together. He was in the OUDS, but by that time I'd given up being Desdemona.' Peter, perhaps not quite understanding the reference, nodded and laughed. 'Good to see you, Sher.'

Sher muttered something incoherent. Could this balding red-faced man really be Bertie Bailey, the school tart at the end of Sher's time at public school? Barebum Bailey, as he was called with good reason, had been a pretty small boy with delicate features, the natural target of a good many seniors. Had he been one of them? He was simply unable to remember, although he recalled seeing Bailey once or twice at Oxford and avoiding him, something that was not difficult because they had come up in different years and were at different colleges. When he came out of this mental daze Bailey was talking.

'Been here a long time, very civilised country, the streets and air are clean. I get over to London sometimes, but it seems so dirty nowadays. Can't bear dirt, don't see any reason for it. I read the other day they did a survey of London hotel kitchens, half of 'em full of cockroaches, chap having dinner found three in his soup, what about that?'

Peter said he hoped they were properly cooked. Sher asked if Bailey was a member of the Silver Blazers.

'Can't say I am, but when I heard you were coming over I thought I must say hallo, have a chat about old times. Peter and I do a little business, and he was good enough to invite me.'

They were placed next to each other at dinner. Sher talked as much as possible to Elise the ever-promising novelist, who was on his other side, but Bailey kept up a flow of conversation about people and incidents of their schooldays which it was impossible to ignore. The need to offer some kind of response to these remarks about people he had not thought of for years made Sher drink more than usual, and the drink seemed to sharpen his senses so that he was aware of anxiety behind Bailey's flux of words. He was not surprised, nor did he take it as a sexual invitation when, while plates were being cleared, Bailey lowered his voice and said, 'Come back with me when this is over. Someone who wants to meet you.' He asked why, and was unprepared for the reply. 'To talk about Sherlock Holmes.'

He began to explain that one of his objects in life was to keep clear of fans who wanted him to sign their books and theatre programmes, or advance theories about what Holmes had been doing in Tibet or just how deep his scientific knowledge had been, when Ulrich got up and proposed a toast to their honoured visitor, who had shown them for the first time on television the true and genuine Sherlock. This proved only one of several toasts to which he was required to respond, not by making a speech, but in Russian fashion drinking with each proposer. During these toasts Bailey remained slumped in his chair, staring at the tablecloth. When they were over Ulrich decreed a change of seating, saying that everybody wanted to talk to Mr Sherlock Holmes – no, he meant Mr Sheridan Haynes. Sher felt his sleeve tugged as he rose.

'You'll come back, won't you? For old times' sake. Please.' He saw the moistness round Bailey's eyes and nodded agreement.

Half an hour later they left. Sher refused invitations from half a dozen Silver Blazers to come back with them for a nightcap, saying that he and his friend were going to talk over old times. It began to rain. Taxis arrived. A man passed by, a small scurrying figure with umbrella up against the rain. About this figure, briefly illuminated in the light from the restaurant entrance, there seemed something familiar, but before he had time to decide whether this was so they were in the taxi, driving away.

In the taxi Bailey talked about himself in a way that left no doubt of his present sexual inclinations.

'Wonderful city, Copenhagen. Open, free, do what you like, nobody cares. I shook the dust of London town off my shoes a long time ago, did I tell you that? Know why? Frankly I found the place was cramping my style, so little *doing*, if you know what I mean.'

'I think so, but you surprise me. I should have thought London was the kind of place where there was a lot doing.'

'My tastes are rather special. I mean, youthful.'

Sher began to regret his presence in the taxi. 'I ought to tell you I not only play Sherlock Holmes but—'

'I ought to tell you, *Bertie*. You always called me Bertie.'

'Did I? It sounds foolish somehow, but very well. Sherlock Holmes was old-fashioned, Bertie, and so am I. I'm not in favour of drugs—'

'Neither am I, certainly not, never use them.'

'Or radical feminists, as I believe they're called.'

'Awful females, I do agree.'

'And while I think people should do what they like in private, I strongly object to them talking about it in detail.'

'Oh, all right. I must say you've changed. I can remember when I was Desdemona and you almost strangled me because I was flirting with Iago. And I don't mean on stage.'

'I don't remember.'

Bailey withdrew to his own corner of the taxi. Sher asked if there was really a man who wanted to talk about Sherlock Holmes.

'Of course there is, you don't think I'd make it up. He wants your help.'

'What sort of help?'

'I don't know.' His voice changed as it had done when he tugged Sher's sleeve at the dinner. 'I talked about you, I often do I'm afraid. He wants to meet you. He's an associate of mine, not exactly an associate, I deal with him sometimes.'

'What kind of dealings?'

'Mostly machine tools. I export machinery to South American countries and he's a representative, has lots of useful contacts. That's what life is, I sometimes think, making contacts, don't you agree?'

They were on a straight stretch of road now, houses on either side. The lights of a car shone behind them. They turned into the entrance of a block of flats and got out. The lights of the following car shone on them briefly, then it had gone by. 'Here we are,' Bailey said inanely.

The apartment was on the third floor. The living room had a picture window looking out on to the street, and a French window beside it led to a balcony. Bailey drew the curtains, then excused himself. Sher looked at the pictures. There was an oil painting of an officer in uniform, hand on broad chest, looking out angrily at the room, and on the mantelpiece below him were photographs of what was clearly the same man out of uniform in a garden, a tall thin woman to one side of him and on the other side a boy of eleven or twelve, the schoolboy Sher remembered. On other walls were school groups from Hunter's, pictures of school plays in one of which Sher recognised himself, and more photographs obviously of a much later date taken at another school. Was a son of Bailey's to be found in them? A lavatory flushed, his host returned. He offered a drink, which Sher refused.

'I call those my memory walls. My father was a regular soldier, a Brigadier-General in the Royal Engineers. I'm afraid I was always a disappointment, he wanted me to follow him into the service, but I just couldn't have endured the life. We never really hit it off. Do you think children are always a disappointment to their parents?'

'I don't know. I have no family.'

'Nor I. You were looking at the other photos, did you spot me?'

He pointed to one of the figures in the more recent school pictures, and Sher saw that he had failed to notice an adult Bailey among the teachers. 'That was my life, I was born to teach. It was taken, oh, fifteen years ago. A couple of years later I was made assistant head. But then, well, I'm a creature of impulse, and I love beauty, I never could resist beauty.'

'Spare me the details.'

'What upset me was that people should say such hurtful things, they forget Jesus said we should all love one another. I think I shall have a nightcap, are you sure you won't? Do sit down.'

'When will your friend be here?'

'Oh, any minute. *Do* sit down, you make me nervous.' They sat in the armchairs, the empty sofa between them waiting for an occupant. 'They were the best years of my life, the ones at Hunter's. Do you know, I could name every member of the cast in our *Othello*, and in most of the other school plays too. Home was awful, the Brig always shouting at me and rowing with Mummy. Going back to school was just heaven, I had the feeling of being wanted. I've not had that for a long time. They were the best days of our lives, weren't they?' He took a handkerchief from his sleeve, blew his nose. 'Don't you ever feel like that?'

'Never.' His recollections of Hunter's were vague, those of Oxford clearer because it was in the OUDS that he had first seriously contemplated acting as a career. His father, a director of a small merchant bank, had accepted the prospect equably, saying he would provide financial support for five years. He had been as good as his word, and when the five years were up Sher was making a rather shaky living. Brinsley had already set up in medical practice, his younger brother David was a youthful don. Just after his father's support was withdrawn he had gone through a lean period, then married Val and, as it seemed by magic, offers of parts flowed in. . .

He had not been listening to Bailey, but perhaps that did not matter since he was still talking about schooldays. Sher looked at his watch. It was after midnight.

The telephone rang. It was on the wall beside the door, and Bailey went across to it. His back was to Sher and he kept his voice low, so that only a phrase here and there came through.

'Of course not,' he said. 'Please don't think. . . I would *never* do such a thing. . . You're mistaken. . .' Then his voice became so low that the words were inaudible. He hung up, turned to Sher.

'I'm very sorry, my friend can't be here.' Sher got up. 'I hope you aren't angry with me.'

'Not with you. I'm not very pleased with your friend for wasting my time.'

'You didn't tell anybody you were coming here? No, of course not. There must have been a mistake.'

'What kind of mistake?'

Bailey's face puckered in distress. He looked, again, as if about to cry. 'I can't tell you how much it means to me to see you again. It was good of you to come out here to Hellerup.

If only you could stay the night – but I know you've got commitments, I'll call a taxi, it will be here in five minutes. About this Sherlock Holmes business. Please understand my part was just to introduce you, that was absolutely all.'

'What Sherlock Holmes business? What are you talking about?'

'I swear I don't know.' He put hand on heart, in a gesture reminiscent of his father's in the painting. 'But some of the people, the people my friend knows, they're not very nice. Not civilised, you understand. Not like you and me.'

'But still you wanted me to meet your friend. What's his name?'

'That doesn't matter now, does it? But I didn't have any choice, over some things I'm really rather committed.'

'To do what your friend tells you?'

'Nothing like that. There was no harm in it, how could there have been, just an introduction.' The bloodshot watery eyes that had once been Desdemona's looked at him imploringly. 'But now apparently something's wrong, and he doesn't like it. I just say I'm nothing to do with it, only a third party. But please be careful.'

4. The Manuscript

Val rang at nine o'clock the next morning. 'So where were you last night? Out with that little devil Peter?'

'Just an odd evening with an old acquaintance. How was your American?'

'Spent the whole of lunch telling me how much he'd paid for a lot of Japanese netsuke and Chinese jade, then made disparaging remarks about pretty well everything in the shop *including* some things he said were fakes, and ended up by saying how lovely it had been to see me again. A dead loss, wish I'd come with you. What's happening today?'

'Just a couple of newspaper interviews this morning, then the reading this evening. Back some time tomorrow.'

'Don't pretend to be bored, you know you love playing Sherlock Holmes. By the way Paul Decker rang, the Prime Minister in person, to say how delighted the Mogul had been to see you, how much he's looking forward to, et cetera.'

It was true that he enjoyed the interviews with the bright young man from *Politiken* and the solemn young woman from *Berlingske Tidende*, and was delighted to be able to play one or two little Holmesian tricks on them. Sher surprised the young man by saying he had spent some time in the north of England, and the young woman by telling her she had trained as a ballet dancer, deductions or guesses he based on the young man's short 'a's combined with the trace of a Lancashire accent in some of his words, and on the masculinity of the young woman's calves and the way she turned, almost pirouetted, as she entered the room. Of course, the guesses might have been wrong, but since they were both right the journalists were impressed. They asked whether the reading was exhausting, whether he felt he was merging his own personality in that of Sherlock Holmes, if he had applied true Holmesian logic to solving the Karate Killings. The questions were familiar, and so was the one the solemn young woman ended with: what did he most like about Denmark? Sher made his standard reply: the people.

Soon after they left the telephone rang. It was Peter.

'Hallo there, did you have a good time with your old friend? That was a bit of a surprise, eh?' He did not wait for a reply. 'By the way, I hope you are free to have a little lunch. That is splendid. And I shall have a guest who wants most particularly to meet you. You have heard of Doctor Langer?'

'I don't think so.'

'You amaze and shock me,' Peter said delightedly. 'He is the Professor of Sherlock Holmes studies at the University of Groningen.'

'I had no idea such a post existed.'

'I can assure you it does. He is here particularly to see the great Sheridan Haynes give his famous reading. And he will have a surprise for you.'

'Another? I'm not sure my nervous system can stand it.'

'How is that? Ah, you are joking. I tell you in advance so it is not a shock to you. In half an hour I pick you up in the foyer, all right?'

In the foyer the little baldish man he had seen last night outside the restaurant sat reading a paper near the door. Sher walked towards him, and the man raised the paper so that only the top of his head was visible. Before he could decide whether to go up and speak Peter was there, and they were away in the little Volkswagen which he drove with abandon, taking his eyes off the road and even occasionally his hands off the wheel while talking about Doctor Gottfried Langer who had, it seemed, published a dozen or more learned essays about Sherlock Holmes's birthplace, youth, possible descent from a branch of the Dutch royal family, and other speculations of the kind that have occupied Sherlockians for more than half a century.

'It distresses me you are not aware of him, but then I think you don't read Dutch. We are damned unlucky, all the little countries in Europe, we have languages nobody understands but ourselves.'

'Gottfried Langer sounds German.'

'Okay perhaps he is German, but has lived in the Netherlands a long time. He is a most respected figure. Here we are.' He pulled up abruptly. 'You see this restaurant is called Fiskaelderen which means the Fish Cellar, but it is also named the Golden Fortune and that is right. By the way, it is the best fish restaurant in Copenhagen.'

Doctor Langer was already at the table. He was smaller than Peter, no more than an inch or so over five foot. A large head waggled about shakily on a pipestem of neck. Little eyes looked at Sher through large spectacles, a hand small and smooth as a child's was placed in his, a thin voice said in good but strongly accented English that the meeting was a pleasure and an honour, and how much he looked forward to the still greater pleasure of hearing the English actor that evening.

'Spare my blushes.' Doctor Langer looked baffled. Peter explained at length, ordered for them from an enormous menu, then sat back and rubbed his hands.

'We won't hang about, I do not want Sher to think I am wasting his time. Doctor Langer, show Sher what you have with you.'

'If you will forgive me, I must first of all explain. Perhaps you know, Mr Haynes, that I have the honour to be the Professor of Sherlock Holmes studies—'

'At Groningen. Of course. The world is aware of that.'

'So.' The Professor rubbed his hands. Sher avoided Peter's eye. 'A little while ago I was approached, and asked if I would look at a Sherlock Holmes story that has not ever been printed. I agreed. I was a little bit excited, but not very much because as we both know there are many imitations written. I expect this will be an imitation. Then I read and I am not sure, not sure at all. So now I bring you the first part, the first chapter I should say, for your attention. Your opinion.' He patted a blue folder beside him.

Sher's heart sank. Peter looked at him, brightly expectant.

'The first chapter. You mean this is a novel?'

'Just so. An unknown novel about Sherlock Holmes, written by Sir Arthur Conan Doyle.'

'You want me to read it and tell you if I think it's genuine?'

'Just so.'

'But you must know as an expert, Doctor Langer, that this is not just unlikely, it's impossible. Why wasn't it published? When could it possibly have been written? Why is there no reference to it in any of Conan Doyle's correspondence? Forgive me for saying it, but the idea is preposterous.'

'That was my own thought when I first saw it. But wait a moment, my dear Mr Haynes, do not be so hasty. There are some answers to your questions. As to why it was not published, that is simple. The story is unfinished, it is perhaps half the length of a novel. When was it written? You will remember that in 1900 Conan Doyle went to South Africa during the war there, as a doctor in a hospital unit, and spent nearly four months in the country. It was during those months that he began the book. He gave it up after his return, when as you know he began to write his history of the war. You ask why it is not mentioned in his correspondence. You will know that when Mr John Dickson Carr wrote his biography of Sir Arthur in 1949 he did so with what we would now regard as extreme discretion. Since then the dissensions among members of the family have meant that no biographer has had complete access to all the correspondence. It is quite possible Mr Carr suppressed, by family wish, letters referring to this manuscript. And there *are* letters, Mr Haynes, letters in the author's own hand, which refer to it. And one more thing. The manuscript itself is *in the hand of Conan Doyle*.'

With quite spectacular skill Doctor Langer had managed while he talked to eat the fillets of smoked eel on his plate.

'Very good,' Peter said, perhaps referring to the smoked eel. 'Now we have Sole Marie Walewska, and perhaps you think you have it before, but not like this. Here is a base of spinach and hollandaise sauce, and with it we have the deep fried shrimps. That sounds good too? And I tell you it is good.'

Sher looked from one face to another. The Doctor's head wobbled on his thin neck, a breadcrumb adhered to his mouth, his mild goat's eyes behind the large spectacles were eagerly expectant. On the other side of the table Peter also seemed to await a verdict. Now he said, 'What do you think?'

Sher sipped his Alsatian wine. 'I think the smoked eel was delicious.'

Doctor Langer looked bewildered. Peter was silent, then burst into laughter. 'Ah yes, I understand. That is the real Holmes reply when he does not wish to commit himself. It is the English sense of humour.'

'Ah, the English sense of humour.' Doctor Langer addressed himself to his fish.

'I think our friend Sher is saying he does not wish to look at the manuscript.' This was exactly what Sher felt, but did not like to put into words. 'I believe you should show him a page, Gottfried, just a page, and one of the letters.'

Langer opened the folder beside him, found two sheets of paper and passed them across the table. Sher looked at them with a curiosity he could not restrain. Both manuscript and letter were in a neat, tidy and readable hand, similar to that of Conan Doyle as he remembered it. He read the first lines of the manuscript:

> It was a winter evening in '87, and I was again feeling some anxiety about the health of my friend Mr Sherlock Holmes. He had recovered from his extraordinary exertions in the spring of that year, relating particularly to the plans of Baron Maupertuis to gain control over the finances of a whole country, that had temporarily broken his health. The strain of a further arduous and lengthy investigation had, however, left my friend pale and listless, lacking interest even in the Agony Columns of the newspapers that in ordinary times were his favourite reading. The second affair had involved the good names of a Cabinet Minister and a beautiful woman, and the world is not yet ready to receive it.
>
> On this evening, looking for something to amuse my friend, I read out loud a paragraph from the *Pall Mall Gazette*. . .

Sher turned to the letter, which was written on stationery that bore the name of a hotel in Durban, and read: 'My dear Mr Fletcher Robinson, You may be amused to learn that I have begun the story we discussed, and that there seems a reasonable prospect of readers encountering Sherlock Holmes again – although he will *not* return from the Reichenbach Falls. I hope to be back in England next month, and to play a round of golf with you. Here we move from chaos to order and the War is, I think, nearly won. Yours sincerely, A.C. Doyle.'

Who was Fletcher Robinson? Sher recalled the name vaguely, without being able to identify it. Langer's eyes gleamed.

'Mr Fletcher Robinson was a correspondent for the *Daily Express* in South Africa, and met Sir Arthur there, although he was not Sir Arthur then, only plain Mr Conan Doyle. They met again when Conan Doyle returned to England.'

'Ah yes, I remember. *The Hound of the Baskervilles* was dedicated to him.'

'Just so.' Sher was awarded the Professor's goatish smile.

'The *Hound* was published in 1901. No doubt that was the story referred to in the letter.'

The large head wagged. 'That is not possible, my dear Mr Haynes. We know from Mr Carr's book and other correspondence that the *Hound* was conceived when Conan Doyle returned to England and went on a trip to Dartmoor with Mr Fletcher Robinson. It was from him that Conan Doyle first heard the tale of a hound that roamed the moor. This letter was written in South Africa, so it must refer to another book.'

'It might have been a short story.'

'But what I have here is the first chapter of a novel.'

Langer tittered, then placed a hand over his mouth as if concealing a belch. Sher's feelings blended curiosity and irritation. At first glance the writing resembled that of Conan Doyle, the opening phrases might have been written by him, and he felt a distinct inclination to read the rest of the manuscript. A specialist in calligraphy, however, might say that the writing was forged, and a Holmesian opening was not difficult to imitate. His irritation sprang from the titter. He was an actor, not an expert on manuscripts. Why should he be shown this material, then laughed at for his ignorance?

He spoke sharply. 'This is a photocopy. Where is the original?'

Langer looked at Peter, who said, 'The manuscript is very valuable. I think there are other letters. Of course they cannot be all carried round in a folder.'

'If I cannot see the original, I should like to know its provenance.'

'This I cannot say. We are no more than agents in

the matter. Gottfried was asked as an expert to look at the manuscript, and I am acquainted with the person who has it for disposal.'

'For disposal? You're trying to sell it for him?'

Peter had broken a bread roll into pellets. He flicked one at a waitress and hit her on the hand. She ignored him.

'I am a good shot, don't you think? I only make an introduction. I say to this person I am meeting the great Sheridan Haynes and he is excited, says he would wish you to see the manuscript. He values your opinion so much.'

'Since he wants to sell it why doesn't he give it to Sotheby's or Christie's in England, or an American auction house?'

'I think perhaps there are reasons connected with the provenance as you call it, but I do not know. I think the person we speak of wishes to dispose of the manuscript privately.'

'If he thinks I'm in a position to buy it he must be a fool.'

'Of course he does not think that. It is possible he has it in mind that Mr Warren Waymark might be interested. You will be giving a performance for Mr Waymark, I think.'

'What makes you say that?'

Peter's china blue eyes widened in surprise. He produced from a briefcase that morning's *Politiken*, which had a picture of Sher arriving at the airport and a couple of paragraphs beneath. Peter pointed to the name 'Warren Waymark' which appeared twice. 'You do not read Danish, so I translate. It says that after the reading in Copenhagen you will be giving another, quite a private one, to the millionaire hermit Warren Waymark. This is not the interview you gave this morning, of course, they have received some preliminary publicity.'

Sher did not know whether to bless or curse the efficiency of Desmond. With regard to the manuscript, curiosity triumphed. He took away the blue folder, and said he would let Peter know that evening what he thought about the story.

5. Farewell, Desdemona

Sher read the twenty pages of photocopied manuscript which made up the first chapter of *The Kentish Manor Murders* with growing interest. They contained classic Holmes ingredients. The client, an elderly irascible Kentish solicitor named Hickson, arrived in Baker Street without notice (Holmes was able to tell that he came from the Romney Marsh area by observing the unique kind of mud on his shoes), and gave a not very coherent account of a client who had disappeared when about to make a new will. Then the client's niece, a beautiful young woman named Olivia Jameson, arrived, with a letter from her uncle saying he had had to go abroad unexpectedly, and might be away for some time.

'The postmark is Paris, the letter is written on the paper of the Hotel Genoa. Your uncle has spent some time in Italy, I believe, Miss Jameson.'

'Several years when he was a young man. But how could you know that, Mr Holmes?'

'The letter is written in a cursive italic script favoured by Italians, altogether unlike our standard copperplate. The nib is one devised especially for italic writing, difficult to obtain here.'

When the visitors had left after Holmes's promise to look into the matter, he rubbed his hands.

'Interesting, Watson, distinctly unusual. I think a little journey is indicated.'

'To Paris?' I asked eagerly. 'Fortunately I am not busy at the moment—'

My friend chuckled, and shook his head. 'No no, Watson, that is the path we are expected to follow. I have in mind instead a visit to that most curious and sinister region of Southern England, the Romney Marsh. And for the moment it must be made alone, and incognito.'

On that note the chapter ended. Sher crossed to the window of his room, and looked meditatively out. He remembered the area from earlier visits. Almost opposite him was the Royal Theatre, where five years ago he had taken Val to see *Parsifal*, and she had become involved in a vivid argument about whether Wagner wrote Fascist music. To the left was Nyhavn, with its bars and small restaurants. In one of the bars they had spent an evening comparing, at their host's insistence, various kinds of schnapps.

Could the manuscript possibly be genuine? The apparently Doyleian calligraphy was consistent throughout. There were alterations on several pages, and as in other Conan Doyle manuscripts Sher had seen they were neatly and clearly made, with none of the arrows leading to long interpolations used by many writers. Sher recognised that he found himself curious, even eager, to know in what disguise Holmes had gone down to Romney Marsh – clergyman, bird-watcher, tramp? – and to read the rest of the manuscript.

The telephone rang. The voice said it belonged to Inspector Jansson, and asked apologetically if Mr Haynes could spare him a little time. When the Inspector appeared he reinforced this note of apology. He was fair, slightly cherubic, so youthful in appearance that it was difficult to believe in his rank. But although young, not unobservant. He noticed the manuscript.

'You are busy, working on your reading tonight. I am sorry to have disturbed you.'

'Not at all.'

'We are much privileged to have you here in Copenhagen. I hope to hear you myself. I was lucky to get two tickets, for wife and self. They are now all sold.'

Sher said he was delighted to hear it. He wondered if the Inspector had come for his autograph.

'My wife is an actress, though only an amateur. Before a performance she sweats, as she says, like a pig, she is so nervous. And she says she must concentrate, can do nothing for some hours before a performance but think of her part.' He spoke earnestly. 'So I understand my call is unwelcome, and much regret it. Unhappily it is necessary.' Sher nodded. Perhaps silence would induce the Inspector to come to the point. 'I believe you are acquainted with Mr Albert Bailey.' Assent was given. 'It is also my understanding that you saw him last night.'

'Yes. We hadn't met for several years. He was at a dinner I attended, and I went back to his apartment.'

'In Hellerup, yes.'

'We had a drink or two, and chatted. Shortly after midnight he called a taxi for me, and I came back here.'

'That is very clear. What was the subject of your conversation?'

'We chatted about old times, when we were at school together. He wanted me to meet a friend of his, but the friend didn't turn up.'

'What would have been the purpose of such a meeting?'

'He said his friend wanted to talk about Sherlock Holmes.'

He expected the Inspector to laugh and say everybody wanted to talk about Sherlock Holmes, but he merely asked the name of the friend.

'He didn't give it. He did say something—' He paused,

trying to remember just what it was Bertie Bailey had said. '—about being careful, his friend knew some doubtful people. Uncivilised, I think he called them.'

'Did it not seem strange, inviting you to meet an uncivilised person?'

'I can't say I thought about it. Inspector Jansson—'

'My name is Einar.'

'Will you please tell me what this is about. Has Bailey done something wrong? Is he under arrest?'

'Not under arrest. His body was found early this morning on the paving below his apartment. He had fallen from the balcony. Did he seem upset when you saw him, did you have any idea he could take his own life?'

The Inspector had been making notes of Sher's replies in a spirex-bound notebook. He now paused expectantly. Sher was conscious suddenly of the room's warmth and of the curious, almost antiseptic smell that pervades all hotel rooms. And, surprisingly, he felt sorrow. Why should he be affected by any emotion at all? He had not seen Bertie Bailey for more than twenty years, and had perhaps never thought of him once in all that time. 'I could name every member of the cast in our *Othello* . . .' – what endless empty vistas were opened up by the words. Farewell, Desdemona, he thought, and instantly reproached himself for such facetiousness. If those schooldays had truly been the best of Bertie's life, how desolate the others must have been. But the Inspector waited for his answer.

He said decisively, 'No idea, no idea at all.'

'He did not seem upset, distressed?'

'He was annoyed that his friend had failed to turn up, nothing more.'

'Very good.' The Inspector smiled, showing a mouthful of perfect teeth. 'My impression exactly. I believe this to be a case of murder. I mention the reasons, they will interest you. One, there are bruises on the back of the head consistent with a blow. Two, marks on the balcony suggesting a struggle took place and your friend tried to hold the railing. Three, you say he showed no sign of being upset.' He paused. 'What do you know of his occupation?'

'He told me he exported machine tools.'

'Quite true. He imported goods also, mostly rugs and carpets from Turkey and Cyprus. Into the rugs, some of them very loosely woven, were inserted packets of cocaine. You may ask why we did not arrest him when we knew of this, as we could have done. The answer is that Mr Bailey was one link in the chain, not an important one. Break the chain, take out the link, and the effect is that of the weed you call ground elder. You know ground elder? Ah, you are not a gardener, I thought you would have been a gardener.' He did indeed look disappointed. 'If you pull at ground elder you take off the top, leave the root. To destroy it you must dig carefully, delicately, follow the trails of the root into half a dozen places. You trace them all and then—' The Inspector's hand moved upwards. '—out they come. All of them, the whole lot. Finished.'

'But it spreads again elsewhere.'

'That is true. Sometimes I think the whole world wishes to destroy itself, with drugs or nuclear weapons. I wish we lived in the days of dear old Sherlock. But we do not. What I have to find out is this.' He put elbows on knees, leaned forward. 'Did Mr Bailey's death have a connection with your visit to him and with this friend who did not arrive, or was it something else altogether, was he perhaps trying to cheat his supplier?'

In general Sher was a cautious man, careful in his habits, averse from taking risks. There were times, however, when he abandoned caution and acted with a recklessness that, as he looked back on it, surprised himself. He could not have said afterwards why he decided not to co-operate with Inspector Jansson by telling him about the Sherlock Holmes manuscript. Something about the Inspector's awed respect made him faintly uneasy, but perhaps that was because he was used to the condescending brusqueness of Scotland Yard's Chief Superintendent Devenish. Along with the slight unease went his curiosity about the manuscript, and a feeling that Bertie Bailey's death had been connected with his visit, and that he should do something about it. This was the moment, also, at which he made up his mind to tell Peter Mortensen that he would like to meet the man who held the manuscript.

'Like the dog that did nothing at night, a curious incident,' the Inspector was saying.

'You have misquoted, as people often do.' Sher detested the misquotation of Holmesian phrases. 'Inspector Gregory said, "The dog did nothing in the night-time", and Sherlock Holmes replied, "That was the curious incident." But I'm afraid my mind was elsewhere, I didn't follow what you said.'

The Inspector looked bewildered and abashed. 'I am sorry, I do not quite understand. What did I say that was incorrect?'

'It is a matter of the rhythm of the prose.'

'Ah yes, I see. It is curious, do you not agree, that you go to see Mr Bailey, he wishes you to meet somebody who does not arrive, then Mr Bailey dies. It seems strange that he told you nothing of the person you were to meet.'

Sher said with Sherlockian loftiness, 'You have my word that was the case.'

'There could not be a little remark you have forgotten? But I should not question the memory of Sheridan Haynes. I shall be glad if you will inform me of anything you may remember, or of course if you hear something more about your friend. You will excuse me for taking so much of your time. I shall look forward with great excitement to this evening.' With the smile of a rueful cherub the Inspector was gone.

If Sher felt at times that he had been too much associated with Sherlock Holmes, through the TV plays and the readings, he still took pleasure in the applause of an audience. The reading took place in the large auditorium of the Falconer, a theatre attached to the Hotel 3 Falke. The acoustics and lighting were perfect, and the packed house was as enthusiastic as he could have wished. The programme was devised to follow the great detective's career chronologically, from *A Study in Scarlet* to the triumphant deception of Von Bork in 'His Last Bow'. Sher of course played all the parts, and adopted four disguises during the show, his Nonconformist clergyman in 'A Scandal in Bohemia' bringing down the house. When the show was over several Silver Blazers came round to congratulate him, and take him to a celebratory dinner in the hotel. He did not see the Inspector in the audience, but perhaps he had been at the back of the theatre.

At dinner he sat between Ulrich and Peter's wife. Velda Mortensen was dark, small and neat. She wore a white, almost backless dress and a green necklace and earrings which, if they were real jade, had cost a lot of money. When she said she had enjoyed the performance it was with a note of qualification.

'Kids' stuff really, isn't it, dressing up and playing detective. That's what irritates me about all this Silver Blazers business, it's just playing games. Do you know they have one dinner each year where they all come as characters in the stories? It gives me the creeps.' He commented on her good English, and her American accent. 'I majored in English at Columbia, my father was in the consulate there. It's all go in New York, wish I was there still. We always claim in this country we've got the highest standard of living in Europe, never add that we live the dullest lives.'

'I can't imagine life with Peter is dull.'

'He's too fond of playing kids' games. That's what a travel agent's doing, dealing in fantasies. With Peter the trouble is he believes them himself. I hear you may be meeting Alvaro.'

'Who is Alvaro?'

'Don't tell me he didn't tell you the name. My God, he belongs in a nursery, that man. Alvaro's got this precious manuscript Peter's excited about. They think it's worth a lot of money, is that so?'

'If it's genuine, yes.'

'We can do with the money, I can tell you that. And you are going to see Alvaro?'

He did not reply. He saw no reason why he should tell Velda Mortensen what he was doing. She stared at him.

'More games, potty little secrets. I call it stupid.' She turned to her neighbour on the other side, a powerfully bearded young man. Sher saw Peter watching them from the other side of the table, thick clown's lips turned upwards. After dinner the little man came up to him.

'Velda is wonderful, you agree? I am a lucky man to be married to her. She is the whole of my life, you know that?' It was in Sher's mind to mention the party in London, but he forbore. Instead he said she had spoken of somebody named Alvaro. Peter rolled his eyes.

'She doesn't care what she does or says, that one. She should not have mentioned a name. But it's okay, that is wonderful if you will meet Alvaro. You have said yes, you will?'

'I should like to read the rest of the manuscript.'

'You are careful, that is good. I call Alvaro and make the arrangement. By the way, he is not here, he is in Amsterdam.' Before Sher could protest he went on. 'He does not like Copenhagen, but it is very quick to Amsterdam, by air it is just a hop. By the way, how sad about your friend Mr Bailey, a real tragedy.' Sher agreed that it was sad. Peter nodded, went away, and came back smiling ten minutes later. 'Everything okay, at eleven in the morning I pick you up from your hotel. Velda comes with us, okay? I have a little other business to do in Amsterdam, she wants to do shopping and perhaps say hallo to Alvaro. They are old friends.'

'Alvaro is Spanish?'

'Oh, I don't think so. Perhaps a little bit, but mostly Irish. His other name is Higgins. Now you'd like to get away from here I expect, had enough of all these boring people, you would like a little action, isn't that what you call it?'

Sher denied a desire for action, and rejected the offer of a lift back to his hotel. On the long walk from Frederiksberg through the quiet, almost empty streets of the inner city, he savoured the pleasure of having held an audience gripped for more than two hours, that sensation of moving, exciting or frightening a mass of people known only to actors and orators. There may be better things in life, he thought, but no other feeling that quite resembles this one. The mystery surrounding the Sherlock Holmes manuscript, the flavour of danger that seemed attached to it, the fact that it was apparently owned by somebody with the exotic name of Alvaro Higgins, added to his pleasure. Had he been foolish not to insist on seeing Higgins in Copenhagen? Supposing he asked clownish little Peter whether his connection with Bertie Bailey involved drugs, would he get an admission or a wide-eyed denial? At the thought of all this his fingertips tingled with pleasure.

This sensation of immersion in fantasy remained with him as he went up in the lift, so that he looked intently at the only fellow passenger, a middle-aged Japanese wearing a trilby hat jammed so firmly on his head that his forehead seemed non-existent. The Japanese smiled, ducked his head slightly, and Sher ducked his own head in response. Still bouncing along on the spring heels of unreality he entered his suite, and in the sitting room was conscious of something wrong. What was it? He turned his head this way and that, sniffing like a tracker dog, balancing on the balls of his feet. He moved quietly across to the bedroom, then the bathroom, saw nothing unusual or out of place, returned to the sitting room and looked round. Drinks cabinet, armchairs, occasional table with ashtray and matches, desk with hotel brochure, basket of fruit provided by the management. The desk, of course, the desk.

He had left the pages of Sherlock Holmes manuscript on the desk. They were not there now. Had a maid moved them? Five minutes' search showed that they were no longer in the room.

The telephone rang.

He picked it up in the expectation that the voice at the other end would announce itself as belonging to Alvaro Higgins, and that the man himself was in the lobby. Fantasy faded as the voice said, 'Hi, it's me.'

'Val.'

'You sound disappointed. Who were you expecting?'

'Nobody, I was dreaming, that's all.'

'How did the performance go? Weeping and laughing in the aisles as usual?'

'It went well. But things have been happening. You remember I said I'd seen an old acquaintance. . . '

Silence was generally uncongenial to Val, but she said hardly a word as he told her of what had happened in the past twenty-four hours. At the end of the recital she sighed.

'What a lovely time you're having. And tomorrow Mr Higgins. Shall I fly out to add moral support?'

'I don't think so. I shall come back after I've seen him. With or without the manuscript.'

'Can't wait to see it. And you. I've been doing a little investigating on my own, talking to Marty Clayton. You know, Patsy Bennett's boy friend.'

'I know Patsy, but I can't say I remember him.'

'Well, Marty's a journalist, spent three weeks at Castle Baskerville a few years back, and do you know what he thinks? Can't prove it, he says, but swears he's right. He says the man we saw is an impostor. He believes Warren Waymark's dead.'

6. *Marty Clayton's Story*

The idea had come to Val as she sat in the kitchen on the morning after Sher had gone, drinking coffee and looking through the stories about Waymark in more detail. The *Banner* had run a series of articles five years back called 'The Secrets of Castle Baskerville'. They told a story similar to several others, of the recluse who had only two interests in life, 'Sherlock Holmes and women' as the reporter put it. He had got a job as an assistant in the accounts department, but had been thrown out after three weeks when he had been discovered telephoning a story through to the paper from what he called the prison complex. The by-line on the story was Marty Clayton, and she remembered that Marty lived with Patsy Bennett.

Patsy was an actress of sorts who had suddenly sprung to celebrity after years of justified neglect, when she played a foul-mouthed but lovable Cockney landlady named Effie Stevens in the very successful soap 'Down Our Street'. In effect she was playing herself, and in the seven years since she had first appeared in the part Patsy had become more and more like Effie in speech and habits. One of Effie's redeeming oddities was a liking for Victorian furniture, which one or other of the lodgers was always scorching with cigarette burns or smashing up. Patsy too developed a taste for whatnots, tallboys and antimacassars. She was, as everybody agreed, good-hearted, but a little of her went a long way. However, she lived with Marty Clayton. Val rang her up.

'Wotcher, me old duck. You got something for me?'

'There's a pretty little jardinière you might like to look at.'

'Got three of the bleeders, love, buy another I'll 'ave to put it in the loo. Anyfink else?'

'Not just now, Patsy, but you know I always have you in mind.'

'Course you do, my love, 'cause I pay top price.' She laughed. Val laughed too, and asked if she could talk to Marty. 'Gone down the boozer for his morning pint. Ask him to give you a bell when he comes back, shall I? Mind, I don't guarantee 'e'll be sober.'

When Marty came to see her in the afternoon he breathed whisky fumes, but was sober enough. He was a red-faced man in his forties, and just as Patsy seemed to be playing Effie Stevens in real life, Marty was a kind of caricature of the traditional hard-drinking tough but tender Fleet Street reporter. His verbal style was as florid as his complexion.

'The story in the *Banner* was all right as far as it went, but it was the one we couldn't tell that would have taken the lid right off Castle Baskerville, my dear.' Marty called all women my dear. 'The bloody lawyers got at us. All right, we said, if we mustn't say it outright we'll drop hints, make suggestions. But the prissy bastards wouldn't wear it, said we couldn't prove anything, we'd have a libel action up our backsides. Let 'em sue, I said, bring it all out into the open. They'd never have gone into court.' He sat back in Sher's armchair, contemplated his scarlet socks, belched. 'Pardon, m'dear.'

'What would you have brought out into the open?'

'Waymark's dead.'

'You mean he died in that American hospital?'

'No, he came out of there all right. We checked on that out

in Montana with doctors and nurses. The doctors reckoned they'd arrested the blood disease he suffered from, not cured it mind, he'd never be running a four minute mile, but held it static. The tale about him dying in hospital was floated by a couple of wide boys who got a lot of mileage out of it. You know what journalists are like, some of 'em.' Marty's laugh was rich, thick, whisky-laden. 'So then he came over here, bought the Castle or rather made the Castle, settled in. Ever heard of Van Helder?'

'Yes, the Prime Minister before Decker. Decker replaced him.'

'I'll say he did. Packed the place with his own people. Van Helder was away a lot on business, Waymark business, and left it to Decker to keep things ticking over. When Decker was ready he got rid of Van Helder's sidekicks Roebuck and Krantz, forced 'em out pretty well at gun point, then sacked some of the guards or pensioned 'em off. Van Helder came back, found the new guards were all Decker's men, wouldn't let him in.'

Val tapped the cuttings by her side. 'You described it in one of these articles.' She quoted: ' "It wasn't a Palace revolution, it was a Castle revolution. When Gene Van Helder returned from his four week visit to Brazil, Bolivia and Argentina he found the drawbridge drawn up against him, and all his attempts to approach the Lord of Castle Baskerville were in vain." Where did that come from?'

'Man named Griffiths, one of the Outer Guards. He'd only been there three months or so when Roebuck and Krantz got the push. Then Decker called all the rest of 'em together, told them Van Helder had been robbing Waymark blind, and the Mogul had appointed him as Prime Minister instead. Hurst – you've met him, just a dummy – well, Griffiths reckoned Hurst was lucky not to be slung out too, he must have known what was going on.'

'You think something *was* going on, Van Helder was cheating on Waymark? How was he doing it?'

'Griffiths thought he was. It was likely enough, they're all villains. Griffiths had been a member of the National Front at one time, but I think they found him too quarrelsome. He was a real bastard for fighting. As to how Van Helder did his fiddling I don't know, but Griffiths thought false invoices, phoney firms, that kind of thing.'

'What happened to Griffiths?'

'He was there almost a couple of years, then got fed up with it, wanted more of the readies, got in touch with me. He helped me to get a job there, but when I was sussed and thrown out they twigged who'd been telling me stories, slung him out too.'

'Do you know where he is now? Can I talk to him?'

Marty chuckled. 'Only in Heaven or the other place. He enlisted as one of Mad Mike Hoare's mercenaries, got himself killed in Africa fighting for a rebel movement against some Marxist Government or other. Mozambique? Might have been Mozambique.'

'What about the others? Roebuck, Krantz, Van Helder?'

'I got news of them, but don't forget I never saw these geezers at the Castle, they'd all got the push in 1979 before my time. Tried to contact 'em, got hold of Roebuck and Krantz. Roebuck was an accountant, set up his own firm, wouldn't talk to me. Then I traced Krantz, living in Morocco when I met him, called himself an anarchist, had plenty of money which I presume he'd salted away before he got the push. Tried to convince me that they, Van Helder and his lot, were pure as virgin forest, Decker was the villain, but I didn't believe much of that. Krantz wanted ten thousand smackers for his story, but the editor thought he didn't have any story worth buying, and he might have been right. I told you they were all villains.'

'Did you trace Van Helder?'

'He's snuffed it, my dear. Went to Bolivia, got in cahoots with some ex-Nazi who was big in the drug traffic there, died in what was said to be a car accident in '83 or '84. There's a suspicion he was knocked off by his partner. The library at the *Banner* keeps a file on Waymark, and they got this paragraph from some local paper. He was supposed to be very smart, Van Helder, and Krantz told me he was a genius, but he wasn't clever enough for our pal Decker.' He brooded a moment. 'Maybe that's not quite right. Krantz told me Van Helder was a gambler, a chancer, great at planning elaborate schemes but not strong on the details. Krantz said he warned Van Helder that Decker was planning something, got laughed at for his pains, Van Helder just wouldn't believe it.'

Belatedly Val offered a drink. Marty shook his head. 'Had enough, my dear, can't put it away as I used to. Like Fleet Street I ain't what I used to be. And nowadays Patsy doesn't like me coming back half-cut, can you believe that? I do what she says, I love that woman.' He blew his nose, looked about to cry.

'You're not playing in a TV serial, Marty.'

'Did I deserve that? Perhaps I did. Every good journalist is a bit of a ham actor, do you know that? I could manage a cup of tea and a sweet biscuit, if it's on offer.'

When he was drinking the tea Val asked him why he thought Waymark was dead. Marty fidgeted a little, head drooped so that double chin was apparent.

'It's circumstantial, that's the word the lawyers always use when they want to keep stuff out of the paper. Before Decker took over, the staff used to see the Mogul sometimes, he walked about a bit in the grounds. Not only the grounds. You've been there, you know there are separate quarters where the staff sleep, restaurant, gym and so on.' Val nodded. 'The Mogul used to go around sometimes, not often, with Van Helder, Decker or Krantz, look in the office, go across to the staff quarters and so on. He never said more than five words to anybody, but they saw him. After Decker took over – finito.' He waved his hand, the teacup rattled. 'Another thing I got from Krantz. In the old days, that's when Van Helder ran the show, Waymark used to get away sometimes. He's even

79

supposed to have gone to the annual dinner of the Sherlock Holmes Society using a false name. But all that was a while back. Again, they say since Decker took charge the Mogul's never stirred outside that door separating his apartment from the rest of the place. In my three weeks I never saw him, and believe me I tried. Makes you think.'

'You say this happened from the time Decker took over, but you don't know that, you weren't there.'

'Statement of the obvious, m'dear. But I talked to people, Griffiths and another guard, one of the secretaries in the office, couple of the cooking staff. They all said much the same thing. Krantz and Roebuck suddenly disappeared, then Decker called 'em in as I said, made his little speech saying they wouldn't be back nor Van Helder either, and henceforth they'd answer to him instead. I'll tell you something else he said. Mr Waymark had been so shocked and distressed by the discrepancies Decker had discovered that he'd suffered a serious relapse, and was confined to his rooms. He's been confined there ever since. One more thing. There was a resident doctor, American named Shefford, been there two or three years. A week or so before the revolution he left, went back to the States. He was replaced by somebody new, name of Prettyman.'

'I've met him.'

'Prettyman's been inside for embezzlement, or whatever they call it out there. He was in a partnership, and used his partners' money to pay off gambling debts. Fine kind of doctor to employ. Anyway, why did Shefford leave?'

Val looked again at the *Banner* pieces. 'You went out to Oregon to see Shefford, but he doesn't seem to have confirmed your suspicions.'

'How the hell could he, when he'd left a few days *before* the balloon went up? He said Waymark was in reasonable health, but when I talked to him he really just played dumb.'

'If what you're saying is right—'

'It *is* right.'

'Shefford would have been appointed by Van Helder.'

'And got rid of by Decker. And paid to keep his mouth shut.'

'You don't know that.'

'I saw the man, talked to him. It was like talking to a brick wall.'

'So you think Waymark was killed, and somebody else took his place. How was he killed? What happened to the body?'

'How? The most likely thing would have been poison, they could easily have fed it to him. Or they might have replaced some of the pills he was always taking with knockout drops. Then a pillow over the face, and goodbye Mogul. It could even be he died naturally, and in that case of course admission of his death would have meant the end of Decker's set-up. The belief is almost all his money goes to charities, certainly not to our Paul. Point is, however he died Decker would have wanted to hush it up. What happened to the body? Couldn't get any firm word on that. One of the guards had a tale about Decker and one of his young toughs loading up a car very late one night and being away for two or three hours, but he could have been saying it for the handout I gave him. No problem, though. They could have weighted him and put him in a river, he could be buried somewhere in the grounds. If I'd had a bit more time – but I didn't, I got chucked out.'

'There's no proof of what you're telling me, it's just guesswork.'

'Spoken like my bloody editor, my dear, or one of the poncey lawyers. That's why they did a nice thorough castrating job on the story, and the *Banner* and I don't love each other any more. Not many editors love old Marty now, cold winds are blowing for freelances, I can tell you. Thank God Patsy still believes in me.'

'Marty,' Val said warningly, afraid that more nose blowing was on the way.

'She's a lovely lady, a woman with a heart.'

'I'll tell you the kind of fact your story's short on. Sher's agreed to give a performance of his show just for Waymark alone, and we went down to see what he was like and look at the conditions in which Sher would perform. And out of curiosity too, because yours wasn't the only news story that hinted at oddities in the Castle Baskerville set-up. Sher talked to the Mogul, Waymark showed him some of his Sherlock collection, and from the knowledge he showed—'

'Easy enough to mug up that kind of thing.'

'So you say, but Sher's convinced he's genuine. If he weren't, why would he or Decker run the risk of setting up this show?'

'I don't know, my dear. My guess would be it's some sort of fiddle, as I've told you several times and now repeat, they're all villains. But one thing I can say with my hand on my heart.' Marty suited the action to the words. 'I believe the Mogul's dead, and that whoever is keeping his chair warm at Castle Baskerville is a phoney.'

7. *The Man in Amsterdam*

As they drove into Amsterdam from Schiphol, passing hamburger and pizza restaurants, Sher thought how much one place now resembled another. Pizza Huts and Macdonald's and a dozen other fast food chains welcomed you in every city and town throughout Europe and America, levis and jeans were unisexual and universal, and the people were hardly more distinctive than the food, the clothes, the new architecture. Within a few years we should live in a completely computerised standardised automated world, deprived of national and racial characteristics, all housing, education, food, clothing, limited by what the computer found permissible. He said something of this to Peter, who listened with a mixture of awe and amusement.

'You know what I think you are complaining about, old man? It is not much like Sherlock Holmes's London. But that was not so good for everybody, I have read. By the way, there were a lot of poor people then, starving some of them perhaps?'

'Of course there were things wrong then. But every country was full of individuals, not of machines pretending to be people.'

Peter repeated the phrase. 'That is very good, I shall remember it. In the meantime, here we are. You will not see anything like this in Copenhagen or in London, I think.' And it was true that the hotel was finely situated, at the junction of two canals. The front was sixteenth century, the interior aggressively modern. 'We just park our bags and leave for our appointment.'

Twenty minutes later they were in another taxi and crossing canals, Singelgracht, Prinsengracht, Keizersgracht. On Herrengracht the driver turned right, the taxi bounced over cobbles. 'Do you know how many miles of canals there are in Amsterdam?' Peter asked.

'For God's sake, you sound like one of your travel brochures.' Velda sat in a corner of the taxi, next to her husband but as far removed from him as possible, looking pretty but discontented. She wore a bottle green jacket and skirt, her white shirt fastened at the neck by a large amethyst brooch. She carried a pair of green gloves. 'It's all piss and wind, what you were saying. We're here now, not in the world of Mr bloody Sherlock Holmes, what does it matter whether it was better or worse?'

'It matters to me.'

She shrugged. 'Tell the driver he can drop me at the Dam. I'm meeting Martine at Di Bijenkorf.'

Peter looked at his watch. 'Eleven o'clock. Perhaps you and she will have lunch with us. We shall have finished our discussion by then.'

She shook her head. 'I've heard enough about Sherlock Holmes, couldn't take him over lunch.'

'Then where will you be?'

'With Martine, of course. We've got things to talk about. I'll be back before dinner, don't worry.'

'You will return to the hotel before six o'clock?'

'I expect so.'

'You cannot be talking until then, surely.'

'You know what you are, Peter? A pain in the arse.' The taxi stopped at the Dam, Velda got out, they drove on.

'It is hell for me, you know. She goes to meet a lover,

84

I am sure of it.' Peter's mouth was turned down. 'I cannot bear it, I love her so much.'

Sher coughed. 'You're not a model of faithfulness yourself, so far as I gather.'

'That is quite different. I tell you, she eats and drinks money, I ruin myself for her. It is terrible.'

'Last night you said you were lucky to be married to her.'

'That is true, I am lucky. But it is also terrible.'

The taxi stopped outside another hotel. The lobby was enormous, the decorations would-be Roman. Busts of emperors from Trajan to Diocletian were placed in niches round the walls. In the middle of the lobby pages scurried around what might have been a scaled down version of Trajan's Column. Peter looked about him. Sher asked whether Higgins was staying here.

'Perhaps. I am not sure. Ah, here we are, we go down. By the way, there is a little surprise for you, another one. In England you have spas, you take the waters in the old phrase, at Baden-Baden also and Budapest, but in Copenhagen you don't, and you think here in Amsterdam you don't too. But the Dutch are clever people. In the past they borrow the land from the sea, and make the water go where they want, now they treat it so it's good for you.' The lift deposited them in an entrance hall with archways off it saying 'Thermal Pool', 'Tub Baths', 'Shower Massage', 'Traction'. Peter bought tickets. A grim-faced woman gave them dressing gowns, towels, bathing trunks, and indicated changing cubicles.

'This is where we meet Higgins?'

'I told you, a little surprise. He comes for massage, we have it too, then we talk.'

'I don't want a massage.'

'But I have tickets for both, you can't waste my money.' The clown's mouth moved upwards. 'Come on, be a sport, you'll enjoy it.'

If Sher had had any idea that Peter might be offering some unusual sexual pleasure it was dispelled by sight of the white-coated Amazonian who briskly ordered them on to marble slabs. Peter lay face down and Sher copied him. A voice beside his ear asked: 'Electrical? Bath?'

'I beg your pardon?'

'You wish electrical treatment or thermal bath? You have rheumatism, arthritis, bad muscles? You want traction?'

'No no, just massage.' He lifted his head, saw Peter laughing at him.

'Head down,' said the voice, and pushed it down for him. A rain of blows descended on his shoulders, then his neck was wrenched sideways and he heard distinct cracks. Fingers dug into the area between his neck and shoulders as if mixing dough. The treatment was much more vigorous than any he had had in England, but after a couple of minutes he found it quite endurable. He had turned over, and the Amazon was chopping away at his thighs when another voice said, 'Mr Haynes. Alvaro Higgins.'

He looked at a long thin head that looked even longer because it was surmounted by a mass of carefully combed white hair that rose to a cock's-comb peak. The man's complexion was dark, his lips two lines. To Sher, whose memory went back a long way, he looked like the actor Conrad Veidt. He wore a dressing gown similar to those handed out to Sher and Peter.

'I apologise for this unusual meeting place. Here we can talk quietly, not overheard.' He spoke a few words in Dutch to the Amazon. She nodded, and a couple of minutes later tapped Sher on the shoulder. He swung off the table and found her holding his dressing gown open. Her sour expression did not change as she said, 'You are not bad, quite good for your age.'

The man with white hair watched, smiling. A moment later Peter joined them, shaking his head.

'She's rough, that one. It was an experience. Her name is Gabrielle, can you imagine?'

Just beside the massage room was a café, empty except for

a fat white-haired woman in a blue dressing gown decorated with red dragons, who had a pot of coffee and a cream cake in front of her.

'You can get anything you like here,' Higgins said. 'After people have been used as chopping blocks by Gabrielle and her friends they usually need strong medicine like good Dutch schnapps. But if you'd prefer a glass of champagne that will be just the temperature it should be, dry as the English like it, I shall join you in it. If you will share a bottle with me I shall know I am forgiven for this outlandish meeting place.'

Sher said yes to the champagne, then steepled his fingers. 'Why are we meeting here?'

'I am staying in the hotel, it is convenient.'

'That is obviously untrue. If you were staying here we could talk in your room, and you would be wearing your own dressing gown, not one of those given to visitors. I deduce that it is not because you don't wish to be overheard, but because you don't wish to be seen in public that we are meeting here. It seems to me likely that you have come to Amsterdam for our meeting, and may well leave as soon as it's over because it isn't a safe city for you. But then Peter said you didn't want to come to Copenhagen, I suppose for the same reason. That doesn't give me much confidence in you.'

Peter started to protest, but Higgins silenced him with a wave of the hand. 'Very acute, and almost correct. I am in trouble with the Mafia over some money which I had a part in laundering. It seems that the process did not make it perfectly clean.' His cheek twitched to show that this was a joke. 'The person involved is a chieftain, which is something less than a genuine chief, and in a few weeks' time I'm sure a chief will have convinced him of his mistake. In the meantime I am careful. Shall I tell you the details?'

Peter looked from one to the other of them. Sher shook his head. The champagne came in a silver bucket, a waiter opened and poured it. Sher raised his glass. 'I drink to your continued good health.'

'I like your sense of humour,' the white-haired man said, although he did not smile. 'Now, can we talk about the Sherlock Holmes manuscript?'

'There can be no harm in talking, as long as you understand that I'm not committed in any way regarding it.'

'Tell me first of all, did you find that first chapter interesting? You would like to see the rest of the manuscript?'

'Yes. But I should like even more to know why you want me to see it. If it's yours to sell, and you want to sell it—' Sher paused, but Higgins merely looked down at his glass. '—why not do so through one of the great auction houses? If you can satisfy them of its genuineness, the price would be high. I'm not an expert on Conan Doyle manuscripts, but no doubt they'd want proof of its provenance and authenticity. How did it come into your hands? Is it yours to sell? Everybody remembers the Hitler Diaries.'

'How could they be forgotten? I'm happy that Peter has been discreet.' Peter shuffled his feet, sipped his champagne like a child at a party. 'You come straight to the point, and I shall give you just as straight an answer. Is the manuscript mine to sell? Yes, but I am not the owner. Why not approach Christie's or Sotheby's, or perhaps an American institution? Because it is essential the sale should be absolutely private. I will tell you why, if our discussion reaches that point. Why ask you to help us? Because we think – I should be less cautious and say we know – the most likely buyer is Warren Waymark, and you will very soon be seeing him.'

'Why not get in touch with him direct?'

Alvaro Higgins's cheek twitched again. 'We have tried. We have written to him, sent a copy of the opening chapter you have seen. There has been no acknowledgement. Mr Waymark is a fanatical collector. If he had read that chapter it is impossible he should not have asked to see the rest of the manuscript, or raised some queries about it. Obviously it has been kept from him. Either he has not been shown the letters and manuscript, or his reply has been destroyed by those who keep him captive. Would you say he is kept captive, Mr Haynes?'

'He's certainly a recluse. I saw no sign of him being a captive. No doubt the manuscript would interest him, but—' Higgins leaned forward in his chair, hands on knees, white eyebrows raised enquiringly. 'There are other collectors. Why not approach them?'

'None of them would pay what we are asking.'

'How much is that?'

'A quarter of a million. Pounds, not dollars or Dutch florins.' Peter sighed gently. 'You think it is too much?'

'One can't put a price on something unique, but I doubt if you'd get anything like that at auction. Less than half of it, I should think.'

'Precisely. But Waymark could pay it without thinking twice. From that will come my commission, and Peter's fee for introducing you. The rest goes to the owner of the manuscript.'

'I still don't understand how you think I can help you.'

'In a few days you visit Castle Baskerville, give your reading. That is correct? Good. If you agree, I will give you the whole of the manuscript – no, I must correct myself, I should say a complete copy of it – for you to show to Mr Waymark. In this way we make sure he reads it. Now, let us suppose he is interested in buying it. We will make an appointment to meet him at an agreed place. We then give him the actual, original manuscript, he pays for it, either in currency or in negotiable bonds. We should be pleased if you were present, to see fair play as you might say.' He paused. 'I think you would be insulted if a fee should be mentioned.'

'Of course there could be no question of payment. But the idea is ridiculous. You must know you are asking the impossible. Waymark never leaves the Castle, hardly goes into the grounds.'

The white-haired man lowered his voice, as if confiding a secret. 'I am aware of that, although I believe there are times when he has left the Castle. I think he might do so again if he knew that was the only way of obtaining possession of a unique Sherlock Holmes manuscript.' More softly still he said, 'And if he knew that Sheridan Haynes would accompany him.'

Two contrary sets of feelings occupied Sher's mind. One was that of the rational man he believed himself to be. This told him that Higgins was at best a con man, possibly something more dangerous, and that nothing he said should be believed without proof. The other feeling was quite irrational, and consisted chiefly of that quickening of the pulse he had felt as a boy when Holmes had cried out to Watson, 'The game is afoot.' There was also the fact that the white-haired man did look more and more like Conrad Veidt, and the prospect opened of involvement in one of those old-fashioned thrillers like *Rome Express* which he had enjoyed so much in youth. He knew very well which set of feelings would prevail, and it was only as a kind of concession to his rational self that he said, 'I can understand why you want me to show the manuscript to Waymark, but not why you ask for a meeting outside the Castle. Why not just go there, see him, and exchange manuscript for money?'

Higgins showed long, slightly yellow teeth. 'You surprise me, my dear Mr Haynes. When we write to Waymark our letter is intercepted. I have only heard the stories, but you know how he is kept from contact with the outer world. Do you really think his guardians – is that the right word? – would allow a meeting of the kind proposed? You know they would not. But now we have got so far let me show you the background, tell you how the manuscript came into my hands, and deal with the matter you call the provenance. I shall be entirely frank—'

'My wife says an opening like that is always the prelude to a lie.'

'Very amusing,' Higgins said, and his cheek twitched. 'But that hardly applies here. What I have to say quite candidly is that on the question of how the manuscript left Conan Doyle's possession I can tell you only what was said to me, I can offer no documentary corroboration. I do not wish to deceive you, I hope that is clear?' His tone was intimidatory. Sher made no reply. 'The work was written when Conan Doyle was living at Hindhead in a house called Undershaw. He hoped that the Surrey air might help to check his wife's tuberculosis. Among the staff was a butler named Faulkner, who was dismissed for dishonesty in October 1900, shortly after Conan Doyle had returned from South Africa.'

The café door opened. Three blond young men wearing the regulation dressing gowns came in, looked round, exchanged raucous phrases in German. One punched another in the stomach, and was rewarded with a kick on the ankle. The waiter appeared, invited them to sit down. All three hooted with laughter, one turned a handstand, they went out. Peter looked after them and said, half-pitying and half-envious, 'Youth.'

Sher said, 'I don't recall that name.'

'So far as I know it is not mentioned in any biography, but nor is that of any other household servant. When this man left he stole the manuscript along with several letters, realising that they had a commercial value. He sold them to a dealer, and the dealer disposed of them to a Jewish business man living in Budapest named Julius Meissner.' With the mention of the city Sher knew what it was his actor's ear had been trying to pick up. Whatever Alvaro Higgins's alleged South American origins, his accent was Hungarian. 'Meissner had a friend named Ferenc Kozma. That friend was my uncle.' He paused. Again the sense of an actor told Sher that the pause was calculated, but the question that followed still took him by surprise. 'How much do you know about Admiral Horthy's régime in Hungary?'

'Not much. He was a Fascist who ruled the country during World War II until the Russians kicked out the Germans. Is that right?'

'Not wholly wrong, but certainly not right. I must tell you a little about Horthy's Hungary if you are to understand what happened.' Sher nodded. Peter wriggled a little on his chair, but when Higgins glanced at him sat still as a child fearful of possible rebuke.

The fat woman finished the cake, ran her fork over the plate to catch the last morsel of cream. Then she got up and waddled out, looking disapprovingly at their bottle of champagne.

'Horthy came to power not during the war but in 1920. He had been Commander in Chief of the Austro-Hungarian navy, which played no very important part in the First World War, and he was energetic in helping to put down Bela Kun's Hungarian Soviet régime. In March 1920 the National Assembly elected him Regent. Why Regent? There was a party in the country that wanted the Hapsburg heir back again, and he was quite ready to come, but the newly-formed states made out of the old Austro-Hungarian Empire turned thumbs down on any Hapsburg. Perhaps somebody else, then? It was agreed that the throne should remain vacant for a while, and Horthy be temporary Regent. However, he had no intention of being temporary. He quickly slapped down two attempted putsches by old Franz Joseph's heir, who called himself Charles IV, and settled down to rule the country.

'First he played off the legitimists, who wanted a Hapsburg back on the throne, against the free electionists who wanted a nationally elected King. Later on, when Mussolini and Hitler came to power, he did more dividing and ruling, again playing off various parties against each other. He juggled with the Smallholders, Count Teleki and his followers, the United Christian Party and half a dozen small near-Fascist groups, and did it very cleverly. All the while he said his own position was temporary, and when the time came he would happily give way to Charles's heir Archduke Otto. But of course the time never came, and Horthy ran through a succession of prime ministers while staying in power himself. Under his rule you did not do badly if you were one of the land-owning aristocracy or a member of the middle class. The Kozma family certainly flourished. My uncle Ferenc owned an engineering firm, my father Laszlo was an architect. Let me anticipate the question you are too polite to ask. In those distant days my name was Andor Kozma.'

'I was not going to ask that. I was wondering what possible connection this could have with the manuscript.'

'You will see in a moment. Our family was friendly with the Meissners, we saw them often at weekends, went on holidays with them, and so on. There was nothing unusual about this, the percentage of Jews in Hungary was much higher than in Germany, and they were socially acceptable. Horthy was anti-Semitic, laws discriminating against the Jews had been passed in the early days of his rule, and just before the war began there were more laws restricting the percentage of Jews allowed to go to university or enter the professions. But there was no active persecution, and Julius Meissner who was a partner in a small merchant bank was able to make himself useful to the régime in various ways. He was particularly friendly with my uncle Ferenc. They shared a passion for Sherlock Holmes, both collected books and manuscripts, but Meissner was richer, his collection much finer. Looking back now I see that uncle Ferenc always resented his friend Julius, who was immensely hospitable, gave expensive parties, was perhaps rather ostentatious about being rich. Of course I did not understand this at the time. I was a boy, eleven years old when Hungary entered the war in 1941 by joining the attack on Yugoslavia. I thought myself in love with my cousin, Ferenc's daughter Eva. Perhaps I was really in love, who knows? She was fourteen. I sometimes think they were the happiest years of my life.'

For a moment he lowered his head, so that Sher saw only the fine crest of hair, then looked up again with the twitch of the cheek that served him for a smile. Peter refilled their glasses but not his own.

'You will not want to hear the story of my adolescence. Early in 1944 the juggling act Horthy had performed for twenty-five years finished, the balls were knocked out of his hands. His Prime Minister, Kallay, had been trying to negotiate secretly with the Allies, and doing as little as he could about German demands for more Hungarian troops to fight in the East, more supplies, stronger measures against the Jews. In March the Germans occupied Hungary, Kallay was taken off to a concentration camp, mass deportation of Jews began. There were many of them, and it was done with the greatest possible brutality, not only by the Germans but by Hungarians who enjoyed taking revenge not only on the rich Jews they hated, but on all of them, men, women and children. The southern frontier zone, Zala, Southern Baranya, Southern Bachka, was absolutely cleared of every Jew, and things were not so much better in Budapest. Even Horthy protested to his puppet Prime Minister, Satojay. It was the beginning of a terrible time. Yet still some Jews got out of the country, not many but some. There was a route through Austria to Switzerland, and it was said that even high officials in the Fascist Arrow Cross were susceptible to bribes.' The thin lines of his mouth turned down in distaste.

'Julius Meissner approached his friend Ferenc. My father stayed clear of politics, but Ferenc always kept in with the right people, was on nodding terms with the Regent, knew the top people in the Smallholders and Arrow Cross parties. Meissner made over to Ferenc by agreement his house and possessions, on the understanding that Ferenc would get him and his family out of the country. They were friends, you understand, and Ferenc assured him the arrangement would be temporary, it would save the Meissner estate from con- fiscation, and after the war everything would be returned to

him. Then Ferenc told his Arrow Cross friends. The whole
Meissner family was arrested, parents and three children, and
deported immediately. They died in Treblinka. Ferenc shared
out the spoils with his friends, although they didn't enjoy
them long. Within weeks Soviet troops were in Hungary, and
the fighting for Budapest began. Ferenc Kozma was killed in
the fighting, and so was my father.'

There was something compelling about Alvaro Higgins's
telling of the story. Sher did not exactly believe it, but found
himself wanting to know more. 'What happened to you?'

'What happened to thousands of others. The Russians
were as bad as the Germans, worse in some ways. They
were like destructive children, smashing things up because
they had never seen them before. Then there was Rakosi
and the People's Republic, and in some ways that was the
worst of all. I got out when I was fifteen.' He made a
gesture, brushing away the past. 'My story is beside the
point. I tell you all this to explain the manuscript. Ferenc
had it, and when he was killed it passed to his daughter
Eva, the cousin with whom I fancied myself in love. She
had no interest in it, no idea it was valuable, simply put it
in a cupboard. She has been twice married, first to a Party
official who was liquidated in the early Fifties after the
Rajk trial, then to a university professor who taught politics and economics, but lost his position when he wrote
some articles questioning the economic policies of the period.
He found the manuscript, realised it was valuable, wants to
sell it.'

'What stops him?'

'Two things. The present régime may be Communism with
a human face as the saying goes, but if the manuscript was
sold publicly they would certainly learn of it and confiscate the
proceeds. I have connections in Hungary still, go sometimes
to Budapest, and Antal Vass, Eva's husband, has asked me
to dispose of it. Now you understand, I hope, why it must
be sold privately.'

'A very interesting story. But of course there is no proof that anything you have told me is true.'

Higgins spread his hands, which were long, thin and delicate, the nails beautifully kept. 'If you come with me to Hungary you can meet Antal, talk to Eva.'

'My dear Mr Higgins, or Kozma as perhaps I should call you, you know perfectly well I shan't go with you to Hungary on any such hare-brained mission.'

'As you please. All I am asking is that you should read the rest of the manuscript, along with the letters Faulkner took, and the statement Eva Vass made a few months ago when the manuscript's value was first understood. If you feel then that you have no wish to be associated with my attempt to sell it, of course you will say so. And I shall be disappointed in Mr Sheridan Haynes.'

'I've said already I'd like to read the rest of it. There's still a point that puzzles me.' Again the white eyebrows were raised. 'Why ask such an enormous price? Surely Eva and her husband would be happy with half the amount.'

Higgins stared at him. 'You are a funny fellow, you know that. Peter, isn't he a funny fellow?' Peter laughed dutifully. 'Shall we say it is because I am not a charitable institution? Nobody who spent those years in Budapest is sentimental about money or anything else. I may have been in love with Eva when I was eleven, but that is a long time ago. You should remember also that I have named an asking price, and an asking price may be subject to negotiation.'

'Where is the manuscript now?'

'The original is in safe keeping, the copy is here in the cloakroom along with the letters.'

Something about the way in which Higgins-Kozma spoke made Sher aware of the man's confidence that the temptations he was offering would be irresistible. Irritation at this cock-sureness was responsible for his saying, 'Do you know a man named Bailey?'

No look passed between Higgins and Peter, but Sher was aware of a fractional pause. Then Higgins said the name meant nothing to him.

Peter said, 'So sad. He was an old friend of Sher, wanted very much to meet him, on the evening Sher came to Copenhagen they went away together after dinner. Then, very sad, shocking, the next day he had an accident, fell from the balcony of his flat. Really a tragedy.'

'He said he had taken me home to introduce me to somebody who wanted to talk about Sherlock Holmes. I thought it might have been you.'

Higgins shook his head. Peter said, 'The world is full of people who want to talk about Sherlock Holmes. Especially to the great Sheridan Haynes.'

'He said some of the man's friends were unpleasant. "Not civilised" was the actual phrase.'

Higgins gave the two of them the last of the champagne. 'I can see you don't trust me, but do I seem uncivilised, Mr Haynes?'

Again Sher found in himself a strong desire to disturb the white-haired man's assurance. He had seen no reason to mention the theft from his hotel room to Peter, but now he said with an actor's deliberateness: 'The chapter Doctor Langer gave me was stolen from my hotel room. That was hardly a civilised act.'

This time there was no pause. Higgins said instantly, 'And one that had nothing to do with me. Somebody else has got wind of the fact that there is an immensely valuable manuscript around, wants to find out about it.'

'Somebody uncivilised?'

Higgins shrugged. Now that he had begun, Sher felt he might as well go on. 'I don't believe my friend Bailey fell from the balcony, I think he was thrown over, murdered.' Peter raised his shoulders, as if in despair at somebody who could have such a thought. 'Inspector Jansson thinks so too.'

This time the look Peter gave Higgins was like an alarm

bell, but the white-haired man did not seem aware of it. He produced a key from his dressing-gown pocket. 'Peter, in my locker you will find two folders, containing the manuscript and the letters. Will you be kind enough to get them for me.'

It was an order in the form of a request. Peter rose, left them. Higgins said, 'And what did clever young Inspector Jansson tell you?'

'Is he clever? He certainly had charm, unlike most of the British policemen I know. He told me Bailey handled drugs. I asked why he hadn't been arrested, and he talked to me about ground elder.'

Higgins's baffled look was satisfying. 'What is that, I don't understand. Is it perhaps a person?'

'Ground elder is a garden weed, very hard to get rid of. If you just pull out the top the rest is not disturbed, goes on spreading. To deal with it properly you have to dig carefully, follow the track of each tendril. Then with luck you take out the whole root. Jansson said Bailey was one unimportant link, and he wanted the complete chain. He thought perhaps Bailey was killed because he was trying to cheat his supplier.'

'Interesting. I should not wish to say anything against your friend Mr Bailey, but do you know, he sounds perhaps not a truly civilised person himself. Mr Haynes, this has been a pleasure. I shall telephone you, to see if we can take this matter a step further.'

Sher sensed a tension in the man not present before, an eagerness to end their discussion. He could not resist asking, 'Why did you want to get rid of Peter?'

The white eyebrows were raised, the cheek twitched. 'There is no deceiving you, you are truly a descendant of Sherlock Holmes. Yes, it is true I wanted to talk privately for a minute or two, yet not to offend Peter. One should always try to avoid giving offence when possible, don't you agree? Ah, here he is. Peter, thank you very much. Mr Haynes, here are the folders. They include of course another copy of that first chapter, which will I hope be proof that I had nothing to do with the theft from your room. I think you will find the whole manuscript interesting. Now I am moving on to the electro-therapy section, they seem to think it might help a troublesome stiffness in my left knee. I shall say goodbye.'

8. The Raid

Sher spent the afternoon reading the rest of *The Kentish Manor Murders*, which took Sherlock Holmes down to the bleakest parts of Romney Marsh, and involved smuggling activities by local fishermen, a body washed up by the tide near Dungeness, another letter from France purporting to be from Olivia's uncle, and a burglary at Burling Manor, in which nothing was stolen except some old walking sticks and a set of fire irons. The manuscript ended with Holmes asking Watson to come down to Burling Manor and report on any odd happenings there, while the detective himself crossed the Channel.

The folders were red and blue, and that was the red folder. The blue one contained Eva Vass's account of how she came by the manuscript, which confirmed the story told by Higgins, and the material said to have been stolen from Conan Doyle along with the manuscript. This included notes apparently made by the author for stories, some of them dealing with Sherlock Holmes, and two letters from the editor of the *Strand Magazine*, one making an appointment to meet, the other saying how eager readers were to read a new Holmes adventure. Both these letters were handwritten, on what appeared to be the magazine's headed paper, and signed with the name of the editor Greenhough Smith.

When he had finished Sher sat thinking, chin in hand. Common sense said the manuscript must be a forgery, and that it would be easy enough to photograph the *Strand* heading, but the desire to believe was powerful, and the spice of mystery irresistible. He was not surprised to hear Higgins's voice when the telephone rang, or to be asked whether he was interested in the story.

'Very interested, although I must tell you I'm still unsure of its genuineness.' Higgins waited. 'But I will show it to Waymark when I see him.'

'Wonderful. You are very kind.'

'I shall tell him I can give no opinion about its being authentic. I shall advise him also that before making payment he should have the actual manuscript tested, paper and ink checked, references verified, the story about this man Faulkner investigated. What I have is only a copy.'

'Very well, I understand.'

'How can I let you know his reaction?'

'You need not worry about that. I shall be in touch.'

'Love is a terrible thing, don't you think?' Peter Mortensen said. 'It makes us suffer.'

Sher thought back to occasions when he had known Val was sleeping with another man or, almost worse, suspected it. 'Sometimes.'

'She was not here when I came back, she had not telephoned. She returned at five o'clock saying she had been all the time with Martine, they had lunch, talked, shopped, et cetera. I do not believe her, but what can I do? We had a big row, she has gone back to Copenhagen. It makes me very sad.' The large mouth was turned down, he looked about to cry. 'By the way, what do you think of Alvaro?'

'He is impressive. And mysterious. But not trustworthy.'

'He is a great man. At one time Velda fancied herself in love with him. But a man like Alvaro has no time for women.'

'What does he do when he isn't selling manuscripts?'

'Different things.'

'Illegal things?'

'What is legal, what is not, I don't know. There are dealers on the Bourse or your Stock Exchange, they move money around, sometimes it's legal and sometimes not, who knows? They are big people, important people, that's what matters. So is Alvaro, a big dealer, an important person. By the way, what do you think about the manuscript? You will show it to Mr Waymark? That is very good, very fine. If the sale goes through I make a bit of money. But what use is money without love?' They were in the hotel bar. Peter ordered another bourbon on the rocks.

'Why didn't you go back with Velda?'

'I have business here this evening in Amsterdam. And then I said I would stay here with you.' Sher had been unable to get a plane back until the following day. 'You come out with me to my business, we go to a good place, real Dutch food, good atmosphere, all right?' He became momentarily cheerful, then lapsed again into gloom. 'She came here to do something of her own, you know, not to see Martine at all, and not because she wanted to be with me. I am damned sad, you know. You think I go with other women because I like them? No, it is because I do not sleep with Velda for—' He shook his head. 'A long time, not for a long time.'

'Peter, why were you alarmed when I mentioned Jansson's name?'

'What?' Peter's look of misery was replaced by one of caution. 'Did he speak of me? What did he say?'

'He told me Bertie Bailey was a drug dealer, and might have been killed because he was cheating on his suppliers. He didn't mention you.'

'There you are then. Of course I don't know any reason.'

'Did you have business dealings with Bailey?'

'Me?' The china blue eyes rolled, the clown's mouth moved downwards in deprecation. 'On my honour as a Silver Blazer, nothing of the kind you think. By the way, however, your friend Bertie was homosexual, and mixed with some unusual people, regrettable people. It may be one of them killed him, I don't know. I tell you what we do now, we forget our troubles and just have a damned good time. We have one more here, then paint a little bit of Amsterdam red as the saying goes, all right?'

Half an hour later they were in the Brasserie de Provence, in a narrow street off the Leidsedwarstraat, near the Leidseplein. In spite of its name the place was whole-heartedly Dutch. The people at the scrubbed deal tables were eating meat balls and stuffed cabbage, and drinking beer. Peter sat facing the swing doors and kept up a flow of chatter, his subjects the failings of his fellow Silver Blazers and the variety of sexual pleasures available in Amsterdam. The place was no more than half full, the clientèle mostly young. They ordered beer from a jug-eared waiter named Joseph.

'We will eat later. It is good here, eh?'

Sher agreed that it was good, although the place seemed to him seedily commonplace.

'You do not have to eat at all, you can sit with a glass of beer for an hour if you like. You could do that in your old Café Royal, I think.'

'That was a long time ago.'

'The man who founded this place was a Frenchman, so he gave it a French name, but everything has always been Dutch. That is a good joke, I think.'

From the interior a woman approached them. She was in her thirties, very tall and broad, with iron grey hair cut in a ragged bob. She wore a man's jacket zipped up in front, trousers and flat-heeled shoes. Her face was flat, heavy, pale, a muscle twitching below one eye. She came and stood beside the table.

'Ilse.' Sher stood up. 'Ilse, this is my friend Mr Sheridan Haynes. He is a great English actor.'

Ilse ignored the introduction, and let loose at Peter a volley of German. Sher could not follow exactly what she said, but understood she was reproaching Peter, and that he was offering her some explanation. He made soothing gestures with his hands, pointed at Sher. Ilse shrugged her big shoulders, tapped her wrist-watch, turned back and went through a door at the inner end of the Brasserie.

'What was all that—' Sher began, then checked himself. He too had a view of the swing door entrance. Through it now came a girl with blue, green and yellow hair done in spikes, and with her the little bald man Sher had seen in the Copenhagen hotel. They sat at a table well away from Sher and Peter.

'Do you know that man?'

'Not at all, no. Who is he?'

'I have no idea, but I'm almost sure I've seen him in Copenhagen. More than once. Shall I go over and ask if he's following me?'

'By no means.' Peter peered at him in alarm. 'Ah, you are joking, I think. There is something perhaps I should say. In a little while I meet some friends here. Ilse is telling me she is here and two others also, and asks why I am not with them. By the way, she says some others are late, and that is true. Ilse does not know these friends who are late, and I have that pleasure, so I wait with you for them.'

'I thought I heard her say there was danger. What did she mean?'

'Ah no no, you are mistaken, you misunderstood. But you are wondering why I brought you here. It is because I wish to be with my dear friend, you understand.' He laughed unconvincingly. 'I remember that jolly time on my visit to London, I want to give my friend a jolly evening here. But I have this little meeting, so what can I do? I tell you. I meet my friends, we have our meeting that takes just a few minutes, no more. I order us a nice dinner, I return, we eat together, find some girls and have nice party, is that okay?'

'It's very much not okay, Peter. It's absolute nonsense.

You've brought me here for some reason of your own. What is it?'

Peter leaned across and slapped Sher on the shoulder. 'You are a very modest man, too modest. You do not understand what an honour it is to be seen in the company of Mr Sheridan Haynes.'

The lighting came from wall brackets and was muted, but still a faint sheen of sweat showed on Peter's forehead. At the next table a young man wearing a T-shirt that said 'Washington Redskins' pushed a packet across to an older man who wore a naval cap at a jaunty angle, above a dark blue blazer with metal buttons, and pale trousers. Naval cap looked briefly at the packet, nodded.

'Peter, this is a place for druggies. I don't know why you've brought me here, but I'm saying good night.'

'You are mistaken. I implore you do not go, it is important to me. Please understand it is quite all right here, cops know about it, they don't mind. I bring you here, it is partly for the local colour—'

Sher got up. 'Peter, you're using me as a cover for something, playing some kind of game. But I'm not playing it, I won't be used.'

'Please, please.' Peter also got up, caught his arm. 'There is no game. I am meeting people here, it is just as I say, but I am worried. Something is not right, I feel it, but if I am with you nothing bad can happen. I have a friend who is a cop, I tell him I shall be here this evening with you. Then they will not dare to do anything. . . ' He stopped talking, sat down again, put his head in his hands.

This vision of himself as a kind of insurance policy, or charm to ward off violence, was one Sher found irresistibly comic. He saw the little bald man watching them while talking to his multi-haired companion. Peter heard Sher's laughter, raised his hands, wiped his face, his thick mouth curled up in a smile.

'I am not much of an actor, I think, what you call a ham

actor. If my friend Sher goes I weep, if he stays I laugh.'

'Nevertheless, I'm going. You will have to weep.'

'Here he is. Jacko, hallo.' In his eagerness to greet the newcomer Peter almost upset his beer.

The man who came towards them was thickset, with a flat nose and boxer's ears. When he spoke his teeth glinted gold. He jerked a thumb at Sher. 'Who's this?'

'My friend Mr Sheridan Haynes, the great actor who plays Sherlock Holmes. The reason for him being here is I am showing him something of Amsterdam.'

'He can piss off.'

'You do not understand.'

'I said he can piss off. The others here?'

'I think so, yes.'

'Hans here? Little sandy sod, looks like a ferret only not so pretty.' He grinned in appreciation of his own wit, looked at Sher. 'Run away, dad. Skip, skedaddle, get on your bike, vamoose.'

'I'll get my coat.'

Peter flapped his hands in unavailing protest. Sher went to the back of the Brasserie. There was an alcove here with coats on hangers. A flight of stairs was beside it, and further back he could see the kitchens, beyond them a glass-panelled door. The jug-eared waiter passed him carrying a tray of food. Sher groped in the alcove for a light switch, could not find one, and poked about looking for his raincoat.

There was a sound of breaking glass. He heard shots from the front of the Brasserie.

Four men came in through what had been the glass-panelled door, carrying revolvers. Two ran into the front of the Brasserie, the other two went up the stairs. Sher moved into the darkness of the alcove. He heard the sharp crack-crack of shots being fired, both above him and in the café. More shots, and a cry. Then silence.

A light shone at the top of the stairs. One of the men who had come through the door appeared there now, with the gigantic Ilse, her arm twisted up behind her. As they moved down the stairs she kicked up at the man's ankle, and when he released her arm turned and brought her knee up to the man's crotch. He cried out, dropped to his knees. Ilse came down the stairs two and three at a time. The man on his knees had a revolver in his hand. Three flashes came from it. The noise seemed very loud.

Ilse took the last four or five stairs in one jump, then lay still at the bottom. Screams came from the café. A man with a chef's white hat appeared from the kitchens, protesting loudly. Ilse lay on her side. The man who had been kicked in the crotch came down, turned her over. She cried out, spat at him as he bent over her. He struck her in the face.

More men came down the stairs, three of them handcuffed. They looked dejected. The plain-clothes men with them had the satisfied air of cats who have just caught birds. Behind them Sher saw, without much surprise, the fresh face of Inspector Jansson. Sher emerged from the coats, feeling a little foolish. The Inspector stopped, smiled.

'Mr Haynes, what a pleasure. I greatly regret that I was unable to see your performance. Duty called me. I understand it is brilliant, which is what I should have expected.'

'You don't seem surprised to see me.'

'Not particularly. Our agent Hans knows your friend Peter. The Provence is in a way under police protection, it can be useful to know who uses it, and who is dealing with whom. Have I said my tenses right? Thank you. But still Mortensen was doubtful, he smelt a rat as you say – English is a remarkable language – and said to our agent he would be with an important man, the great actor Sheridan Haynes. So you see there was nothing clever on my part. When I finish here we should have a little talk. Ah, here is a casualty, I think.'

They were back in the central part of the café. The people at the tables had gone, including the little bald man and the girl with multi-coloured hair. The jug-eared waiter and two of the agents were gathered round something on the floor. Apart from them, another man stood talking to the handcuffed Jacko. Suddenly Jacko's flat inexpressive face was animated, turned into a machine spitting out abuse. For a moment Sher thought he was the object of it, then realised it was the pale sandy man who stood just behind him. Even before Jacko called him by name, coupling the name with a flow of four-letter words, Sher realised that the thin sandy man with a pointed nose and alert small eyes must be the Hans who was like a ferret but less pretty. Then he turned back to the group and to Jansson, who was kneeling beside the figure on the floor. Now he straightened up, and began to ask questions. Behind him Peter Mortensen lay, face up, the clown's face fixed in a grin. Blood stained his shirt and jacket.

The sight of sudden death is always disturbing. Sher dropped to his knees as Jansson had done, called Peter's name, touched the warm face, incredulous that there could be no reaction. He felt a hand on his shoulder. Jansson's face looked down, the cherubic features solemn.

'There is nothing to be done.' He made a gesture at Jacko's departing back. 'He started shooting, and two of my men shot back. None of them would win a prize in a shooting gallery. Your friend Mr Mortensen got in the way of a bullet. Such things happen.'

'He was not my friend, but I liked him. I am sorry he is dead.'

'So am I, although I do not think he would have told us much. I will take you back to your hotel, we can talk on the way.'

'Yes. Perhaps you will tell me what a Danish policeman is doing in Amsterdam.'

'I am Danish, but I did not say I was attached to the Danish police. You made an assumption without facts, I am afraid. I am attached to Interpol.' In the back of the police Mercedes Jansson explained. 'You remember I talked about getting to the roots of the ground elder? That was the object of the exercise. This drugs ring was operating with the help of bribed Customs officials and policemen as usual, and to arrest one or two of them, or your other friend Mr Bailey, would have meant little, almost a failure. We got our agent Hans into the ring four months ago, and Oberkommissär Müller who was directing the operation offered himself as a man ready to take bribes if they were big enough. Tonight we shall have a fine haul of cocaine being taken through Amsterdam Customs on the way to Scandinavia and Britain, but the object was to get the main agents responsible for distribution. We have several, including Mortensen – most of the couriers in his travel agency carried drugs which went to dealers in various countries, some of them quite innocently. So it has not been bad, but still the operation has not been fully successful, I am not sure of the reason. Tell me, why did you come here to Amsterdam?'

He listened with interest as Sher told him of the manuscript, and at mention of Higgins's name smiled slightly.

'You know him?'

'I know *of* him, by that name and some others.'

'He's the chief of the ring?'

Jansson's laugh was fresh as a schoolboy's. 'There is no chief in the sense you mean, my dear Mr Haynes. In Paraguay, Colombia, Bolivia, there are business men, multi-millionaires. Perhaps they are what you call the chiefs, but they would say they are business men, they have nothing to do with the people responsible for the processing and shipment of heroin, cocaine or cannabis. And they are business men, as they have grown rich they have become owners or part owners of multi-national companies, they have founded banks, their representatives are on the boards of hundreds of respectable firms. The drug business is a hydra that will never be finally conquered by Hercules. Tonight we have scotched just one little head, not even quite that. Higgins left on a flight for Brazil this afternoon. We didn't arrest him because it would have damaged this evening's operation.'

'I am afraid I may have been partly responsible. When we were talking I told him you had come to see me about Bailey's death.'

'Do not concern yourself. I had no idea you would see Higgins, and did not the great detective himself say it is human to err?'

'As soon as I mentioned your name he got Peter Mortensen out of the way, so that he shouldn't hear what we said. Does that mean he deliberately sacrificed Peter?'

'And the others, yes, or at least very possibly. He realised his operation here was blown, and decided to cut his losses.'

'What a ruthless bastard.'

'Drug dealers, Mr Haynes, are not as nice as you or me. But here is your hotel. Before we part tell me a little more about this wonderful manuscript.' He listened attentively. 'You realise it cannot be genuine, you are being used for some purpose.'

'Perhaps. But I can't for the life of me think what.'

'This is not at all my concern, you understand, but I will give you some advice. It is that you should have nothing more to do with this manuscript. When Mr Higgins approaches you again, you should say so.' He held out a hand. 'And now let me say how great a pleasure and honour it has been to meet you, and again how much I regret having missed your classic performance. Sherlock Holmes has no greater admirer than Einar Jansson.'

Even while he went up in the lift to his room, Sher knew he would pay no attention to the advice. On the following day he returned to London.

9. At Castle Baskerville

Paul Decker came to the weekly meeting with Gordon Hurst after a dozen lengths in the bath in which he left Jimmy trailing, and a work-out in the gym. He saw Hurst's pallor with satisfaction.

'So what's new, Gordon?'

Hurst always brought with him a black file and a small notebook, and his report was preceded by a cough so brief that it was almost a hiccup. He opened the notebook and took a ballpoint pen from his inside breast pocket. Then he opened the file and began to read his report. These actions never varied.

The report consisted mostly of the petty complaints about conditions, behaviour and food inevitable in a closed society like Castle Baskerville. Sometimes there were marital problems when affections were transferred, and during the winter turnover of staff was high. Hurst dealt with such things, and indeed with everything internal that had no direct link to the Mogul himself. Decker's attention wandered as he heard - stories of food thrown to the floor in protest against the repetitious menu, crowding in the baths, demands for more recent films. A catering assistant had been dismissed for sneaking out to a local pub, although 'local' was a misnomer, since the nearest pub was three miles away.

Hurst turned a page, and said in a voice dry as ashes, 'Eric Malby, Outer Guard. Slackness in dress, bad time-keeping, rudeness and drunkenness. Already warned twice, second time fined. Dismissal recommended.' He was about to continue when Decker stopped him.

'Wasn't he brought in by Jimmy?' Hurst consulted the file and agreed. 'Then let's see what Jimmy says.' He picked up a telephone.

Jimmy, when he came in, was unimpressed by the account of Malby's misdeeds. 'I never said he was a choirboy. He used to be a night club bouncer, what do you expect? Who's been complaining?'

Hurst looked at the file again. 'The Gate Officer, Brian Watson.'

'The one who thinks he's playing county sheriff all the time. I wouldn't pay attention.'

'Nevertheless he is Malby's superior. He complains of persistent lateness, in particular when the Outer Guard is being changed. Twice Malby was found asleep in the Gate House when on duty.'

Jimmy shrugged. 'He's used to punching chins, not clocks. And he's not only handy with his dukes, Eric, I'll bet he can shoot straighter than Sheriff Watson. He's never learned to say please and thank you, does it matter?' Hurst looked at him blankly. Decker smiled and said, 'Thank you, Jimmy.'

When the door had closed Hurst said, 'There have been other complaints about Malby's rudeness, the most recent when Mr and Mrs Haynes came.'

'You don't think Watson just dislikes Malby, wants to get rid of him? There's something in what Jimmy says.'

Hurst's voice was lowered, deferential. 'Slackness, drunkenness, bad time-keeping. It's for you to decide, PM.'

'Just so. Speak to him yourself. Tell him any more trouble, he's out.' Hurst made a note. 'About Mr and Mrs Haynes. You know he's coming to give his Sherlock Holmes readings.

Have you heard anybody discussing it, saying they'd like to see it?'

'No. So far as I am aware nobody knows the date. I don't know it myself.'

'Next Friday.' Another note. Decker said suddenly, 'Whisky and soda, Gordon?'

'I beg your pardon?' Hurst looked at his watch. 'It's eleven o'clock.'

'Just wanted to see your reaction. Have you ever done anything out of the routine? A right time for everything, is that it?'

'Yes, I think I should agree with that.'

'What do you get out of it, Gordon? I'd really like to know. You've been with the Mogul, how long is it, twelve years?'

'Not quite. It will be twelve years in March.'

'You get well paid, right, but you don't spend the money or I don't see any sign of it. You're not interested in women, or if you are I've missed that too. You don't gamble like Dave Prettyman, you don't collect books or butterflies or coins or anything else, or if you do you never mention it.'

'My father is an invalid. I support my parents, as I am sure you know.' An information sheet was prepared on every employee's background when they were engaged, and regularly updated.

'True enough. But still—'

'And I am better paid than I should be in any equivalent job. I deal with the staff. It might be said that I run Castle Baskerville, PM.'

Decker looked startled for a moment. 'I suppose it might. Under my instructions.'

'Of course.'

'And you enjoy that?'

'I do. And I have always understood that I have no connection with the Mogul's well-being, mental or physical. That is outside my remit.'

'Outside your remit,' Decker said wonderingly. 'Gordon, you are too much. Don't get me wrong. Your services are valuable, and I hope I show I rate them that way. I'd just feel easier if I knew what you get out of it, apart from money. Since live birds don't interest you, why not start to collect stuffed ones? It would be a weight off my mind if you did.'

Hurst did not reply, but closed the file and snapped an elastic band round his notebook. Decker watched in amusement and irritation. The weekly meeting was over.

'My uncle Nils was a hard man. I'd get home from school and show him the bruises on my legs and back – they'd get me down, four or five of them, pretend I was a wild animal, that was the game. I was a late reader, I ask you how could I be anything else spending three years on the road with my dad. Not that I regret it, mind you. He was a spellbinder, my dad, could have sold refrigerators to the Eskimos or coal in an African desert. I owe him a lot, though in another way I got no debts to anybody, had no help, it was all my own initiative. That's what you need for success, initiative. I ever tell you they called my dad the Tongue?'

'Yeh, you told me.' They were in the Mogul's bedroom, the curtains fully drawn, the only illumination an electric night-light in a corner of the room. He lay on the bed in pyjamas and dressing gown, Polly Flinders sat on a chair beside the bed. She had taken off her dress, and wore only bra and panties. It was very warm in the room.

'Uncle Nils said I had to take it. They do it to you, you do it back to them twice as hard. That was good advice, and I never forgot it. If you do that, he said, you'll get to be top dog, and that's what I became. That's why they called me the Mogul, even the President. When I talked to him he said to me, "Mr Waymark, I know they call you the Mogul, nobody ever called me that." The President of the United States said that to me, and asked if I could do him a service. It was a little matter of disestablishing somebody, he said. I like that word, Mr President, I told him, disestablishing, you need not say any more, just mention a name. You know what it means, it means whoever was causing trouble just isn't around any more. I'll tell you a story about the Garment Workers' Union, the way they threatened the Mogul and just what he did, played along with 'em and fairly made fools of them.' She had heard the story, or others like it, a dozen times but she did not say so. At the end of it he said, 'It's cold in here, come and lie beside me, just beside me, not touching, you know I can't bear that.'

It was a double bed and she lay on her back, arms folded, staring up at darkness.

'Pull up the covers.' She did so. 'Here we are, snug as bugs in a rug. And I feel the warmth seeping from your healthy young body into my old bones.'

'You don't always say that. About not touching.'

'It is a question of sensitiveness. Every man out of the ordinary, a man who's something special, top dog you might say, has something specially sensitive in his nervous system. When I'm excited – and I mean emotionally, not physically, that isn't important – it is as if I had been stripped of skin. The flesh is raw, a touch on it would make me scream. At other times I can manage the physical, I can be eased.'

'I've noticed.' She laughed, but knew she should not have done as the body beside her stiffened slightly. 'I know you have these upsets, Warry. I'm good for you, aren't I?'

'It helps to talk, let my thoughts run freely. I need a listener, and Polly is a good listener, one of my best.'

'These upsets, you seem to have a lot of them lately. I just wondered—'

'What did little Polly wonder?'

'Are you taking some special medicine? Some stuff you didn't use to take, know what I mean?'

'What a funny little Polly Flinders it is. The Mogul takes six different medicaments every day, you know that? Every few weeks Dave Prettyman tries something new.'

'Yeh, I didn't exactly mean that.'

'What did pretty Polly mean?'

'Something Lavender gave you, not Doctor Prettyman. Is there anything like that?'

'Say what you mean, Polly.'

'I dunno. It's just, some of the things he says, he says funny things, like he was planning something.'

The thin voice sharpened. 'What things does he say?'

'I told you, I dunno.' She flung back the covers, got out of bed. 'I'm too bloody hot, this room's stifling.'

The voice was sharp, intense, inexorable. 'I think you have fallen out with your negro lover, Polly Flinders. Perhaps he is too potent for you, too urgent in his demands, that is said to be true about men of his race. I had a little black listener once, what was her name? Never mind. You've quarrelled, so you are making up these tales.'

'Think what you sodding well like. I said it because I was fond of you, that's why.'

He pressed the bell push beside the bed. Lavender came in.

'I feel a migraine coming on, Lavender. One of your pads, as quickly as you can.'

'Okay, boss, one minute. You want Polly to stay?'

The figure on the bed raised a hand, let it fall limply. Polly made a sound that might have been a snort of derision or a sob and left, closing the door with a slight thud. The figure on the bed winced. Lavender went out, returned with a pad that smelt of vinegar and ether, placed it gently over eyes and forehead. The figure on the bed sighed. A minute passed.

'Are you still there, Lavender?'

'Still here, sure. Any better?'

'Every nerve in my body is jangling.' Beneath the covers he twitched slightly. 'Lavender, I want you to know I appreciate your help this past twelve months. Is it twelve months?'

'Twelve come the end of October, right.'

'You have made a sick man's life easier. What people do

not understand is that I cannot endure a raised voice. You are considerate, Lavender. You know I am not a well man, there are times when I must not be bothered.'

'That Polly been playing you up? She don't mean it, you know that, she told me she admired you more than any man she ever met.'

'Did she say that, Lavender?'

'Sure did. And meant it. No cause to say it to me unless she meant it.'

'There was a time when women worshipped the Mogul. But that was long ago.'

'Just you don't get out and about, don't see so many. Those you do see, though, the old magic still works.'

'All I need is a good listener, one who understands and sympathises. I must have that.'

'Yes, boss.'

'You know I am always curious, I must know things. Does Polly satisfy you sexually? And you, you satisfy her?'

There was a pause before the nurse said, 'Sure.'

'She says absurd things sometimes, she makes scenes. I cannot have scenes, Lavender. If Polly makes scenes I must let her go.'

'I'll talk to her. I tell her she's brought on your migraine, you know what that girl'll do? She'll cry her eyes out, want to say sorry.'

'This pad is wonderful. I can feel the pain draining away, the hammer blows changing to gentle taps at the back of the brain. Unscientific, but that's the way it feels.'

'I'll be back in a few minutes, change the pad.'

When the nurse returned fifteen minutes later, however, his charge was asleep.

Lavender did talk to Polly Flinders. That evening after dinner they walked in September twilight across the grounds to the residential complex where Polly slept. Lavender stayed in the Castle and in the Mogul's suite.

'We goin' up to your room?' When she said not that

119

night he grabbed her arm. 'What you mean, not tonight? You avoidin' me, are you playin' around with somebody else, is that it?'

'Of course not. I'm tired and I've got the curse. You're hurting my arm.'

He still held her arm, but relaxed the pressure. 'And another thing, you been saying things about me. What things?'

'Telling him things? That creep?'

'So he's a creep, all right, but what harm does it do to sit there and listen to him?'

'And lie down with him. And when he can manage it do what he calls massaging him. I'd sooner he wanted to put cuffs on me, hang me on a hook or something, it'd be more lively.'

'You get well paid.' She shrugged. 'You were pleased enough when I got you in.'

'That was then, this is now.'

'I been here twice the time you have, saying yes boss, no boss, how's the head today boss. You think I like it?'

'You're you and I'm me, that's the difference.'

'Listen, we said we'd do it for a few months, have the cash to buy us a flat. That's still the idea, okay? It's still my idea, yours too, right?'

'I suppose. But I still don't want you up tonight. Besides, you're supposed to be within call of the creep.'

'He's asleep, will be for a couple hours yet.'

She went on saying no, and at last he turned on his heel. She stood watching until his figure was lost in the darkness of the Castle, then went up to her room. There she was joined later by the Gate Officer, Brian Watson.

Decker sat in the room where he had received Sher and Val, listening to the small bald man's account of what had happened in Copenhagen and Amsterdam. When he came to the raid on the Brasserie Decker questioned him closely about what the people in the café had looked like, and just what had happened.

'I was in there with a bint I picked up, protective colouring you might say, but Haynes spotted me.'

'He recognised he'd seen you here?'

'Don't think so. The idea about the disguise worked.'

Bogan was a private investigator, a one-man agency Decker used occasionally when he was doubtful about people he was dealing with, either in the various Waymark enterprises or at the Castle. He had no suspicions of Haynes or his wife, but the idea of reading to an audience of one was certain to be publicised, and who knew what undesirable figure might attach himself in some way to the actor's coat tails in the hope of gaining access to Castle Baskerville? The idea of a reverse disguise, of showing himself to the actor falsely bearded and wigged so that his actual clean-shaven baldness should not be recognised had been Bogan's own. It had seemed to Decker merely silly, and indeed he did not look for mental acuity in Bogan, but for faithful adherence to instructions. However, if the detective was to be believed Haynes had not identified him.

'There was a hell of a hullabaloo going on, shooting, somehow the Dane who'd brought Haynes in got hit. And more stuff going on at the back, didn't see what happened there. The bint I'd brought in was screaming blue murder and I thought I'd better clear out. I'd found out the flight Haynes was booked on back to London, made sure he took it, thought I'd better not be on the same flight. That's about it.'

'Tell me again about Copenhagen. When you followed Haynes and Bailey to Bailey's apartment, you think you were followed yourself?'

'Sure I was, though I don't think it was me they were interested in, more likely what Bailey was doing with Haynes. They were in one cab, I was in another, and this car was behind me. When they got to Bailey's place I told my driver to slow down, make sure where they were going. That would have been pretty obvious to the car behind. I didn't know he was following me till he slowed down too, almost stopped, then speeded up and passed my taxi.'

'And you took these from Haynes's room in Copenhagen.' Decker looked at the pages of manuscript. 'Why not photograph them?'

'Didn't think I had time. Besides, didn't have my camera with me.' Decker looked at him. 'You never told me there might be copying of documents, that sort of stuff, I just went in to have a looksee.' He said virtuously, 'Couldn't risk him finding me in the room.'

'But by taking them away you told him there'd been a thief in the room.'

'It's only a bit of a book, wouldn't have taken it if I'd known what it was. I did what I thought. If you'd told me about the kind of stuff I might come across maybe I coulda done something else.'

Decker was almost always polite. He thanked Bogan, and made a mental note not to use him again.

When he was alone he reread the chapter. He had never read the Sherlock Holmes stories and knew little about Conan Doyle, but he remembered a letter that had come not long ago from somebody named Langer, about a manuscript he had for sale. All correspondence addressed to the Mogul was seen first by his Prime Minister. It consisted chiefly of begging letters, many telling harrowing stories, some invoking past acquaintance in America, a few making veiled or open threats to reveal discreditable events in the past. Most of the latter were destroyed unanswered, to a few a reply was sent saying that Mr Waymark had no recollection of the events mentioned, or that any further letters would be placed in the hands of lawyers or the police. Doctor Langer's letter had not been passed to the Mogul because it was the kind of thing likely to excite him undesirably. Castle Baskerville was a cocoon in which, most of the time, the Mogul was content to remain safely wrapped, out of contact with the outside world. Occasionally, however, perhaps twice a year, he seemed to feel a need for exposure to those very dangers and terrors from which the Castle gave protection. The visit to the Sherlock Holmes Society was long ago, but there had been other escapades since. A letter from a young woman who claimed to be the daughter of an old flame of the Mogul's in Montana had been smuggled through to him, he had made an appointment to meet her, bribed an Outer Guard to drive him to Tiverton station, taken a train in the wrong direction and telephoned from Penzance police station, where he had taken refuge. That affair had been hushed up successfully, only vague stories appearing in the press, and of course the Outer Guard had been sacked immediately, but Decker had no intention of risking such a near catastrophe again.

Yet he realised that the kind of excitement which had prompted the Penzance escapade was bound to recur, and tried to make provision against it, so that when the Mogul mentioned the idea of a special performance of the Haynes readings he had applauded it, and set out to make the arrangements. Yet such ideas always carried with them the possibility of some trick being played, and here was this manuscript to prove the fact. No doubt it was a forgery, and the forger was using Haynes as a stalking horse. Probably Haynes would show the manuscript to the Mogul. Did it matter?

In terms of his own interests, as far as Decker could see, it did not. Somebody was trying to sell this manuscript, and whether it was genuine or not interested Decker very little. If it had come up for sale in the usual way in an auction room he would have had no objection to the Mogul making a bid, although there had been something in the tone of that original letter from Doctor Langer, a readiness to come over in person and talk to Mr Waymark, that disquieted him. Thinking it over, he came to the conclusion that it was probably this Doctor Langer who was using the actor as an agent. Haynes would show the manuscript, either the chapter of which Decker held a copy or the whole thing, to the Mogul, and tell him what was being asked for it. That could do no harm. As for the drug affair, it seemed of no concern to him.

Decker made visits to London twice a month, and one was just about due. He had to work out the final details of a siphoning of assets from a couple of Waymark companies to a newly acquired one with George Darnley, the lawyer who looked after the whole of what was still a considerable empire. Decker was in frequent touch by telephone, but believed it was important he should be seen in person. When he was away Gordon, ever-reliable Gordon, minded the shop. And who minded the minder? Jimmy along with Vince, who had been a car salesman, a heavyweight boxer and a cinema manager in his time. Who took care of them? They were too thick to try anything, and had been chosen partly for that reason. Paul Decker liked to think he was a man who did not leave much to chance. There seemed no reason why he should not stay up for a couple of days, and spend them with Anna Ridley.

Decker had never married. Anna was his mistress, a ridiculous word as it seemed to him, since he was ready and indeed eager to make her his wife. She was in her thirties, several years his junior, fashion director of a women's magazine. The relationship had lasted some time, and soon after it began she had come down to Castle Baskerville with the idea that she would give up her job, marry him, and live there permanently. After a couple of weeks she fled, saying it was like being in a jail where the warders were also the prisoners, and that Paul must be mad to endure it. But Decker knew that he not merely endured but enjoyed being the effective ruler of a commercial empire. He was, he said to her, rich but honest. Whoever came after him would probably be like Van Helder, and rob the Mogul blind.

'But to take orders from a man like that – just the sight of him made me shudder.' She had seen the Mogul only once, on her arrival at the Castle, and said that was more than enough.

'I don't take orders. But if that's how you feel—'

'It is how I feel.'

They both knew it would be pointless to suggest that he should leave, yet it was not the end of their relationship. Sex, Decker had long known, was less important to him than power, and he suspected that Anna greatly valued her independence. Did she have another lover, perhaps more than one? The possibility left him untroubled. He telephoned her always when going to London, and generally stayed at her flat near Regent's Park. If that was not convenient she told him so, and he accepted it. But that did not happen often and now, when he telephoned and said he would be in London and hoped she would be free for dinner, she said that would be fine. Her voice, as ever, was cool. He liked that coolness.

10. People in London

Nobody could have said that Desmond O'Malley did not work for his clients, especially those like Sher who seemed to him in need of publicity. It was in pursuit of duty that he took Harry Morley, features editor of the *Banner*, out to lunch, and told him about Sher's impending visit to Castle Baskerville. What Desmond proposed was a ghosted article with Sher's name attached to it, called something like 'I Played to an Audience of One'. Morley was a thin, miserable-looking man with a sniff which he used as critical comment. He sniffed now.

'He's not much of a name. One of yesterday's actors playing costume drama.'

'Not much of a name.' Desmond was scandalised. 'For a whole generation Sher *is* Sherlock Holmes. And putting on a show for one person, that's unique.'

Morley dabbed at his fillets of sole in a dissatisfied manner, then pushed the plate aside. Desmond, a hearty eater, no more than halfway through his steak tartare, could hardly bear it.

'Unusual, I agree. Would he wear it? I hear he can be awkward.'

'Sher's his own man, thoroughly independent.' Morley sniffed. 'An interview might be easier than an article. But leave that to me, I can talk to Sher, make him see it's in his own interest.'

'It certainly would be.'

You miserable bugger, Desmond thought, the things I do for clients. Reluctantly he abandoned the steak tartare. 'Harry, do I detect a lack of enthusiasm? If you think there's nothing in it for the *Banner*, fair enough, I'll go somewhere else. I came to you first.' Both of them knew this was because the *Banner* was the best prospect.

'I didn't say that, just I see problems. You're a great salesman, Des.' It sounded like a death sentence. 'But I'd have to get an okay from the man up there. Suppose I say yes, and it turns out to be a turkey.'

'I think you'd sooner opt out of it. Say so, no hard feelings.'

'Des, I didn't say that. I just need a little time to consider. When did you say he performs?'

'I didn't. Next Friday.'

'You mentioned lighting problems. Will they be settled in time?'

'Of course they will. We've arranged for the technicians to go down on Thursday, Sher says it won't take more than a couple of hours. What about a look at the trolley? Very good profiteroles here.'

'I envy you your digestion. Just black coffee. I'll give you a call by six to say yes or no, all right?'

Desmond said it would be all right. He regretted missing the profiteroles. When he got back to the office he rang Sher and received a discreetly edited account of what had happened in Copenhagen and Amsterdam, to which he did not pay full attention.

'Great,' he said. 'Sad about your friend, but great, great, publicity is the name of the game. Now, don't take this as firm, it's not fixed yet, but the *Banner*. . . ' He gave an account of the lunch, in which Harry Morley had been excited by the prospect of an article by Sher about the extraordinary experience of performing for just one person. When Sher said he understood perhaps half a dozen others might be present, the agent brushed aside the words.

'Essentially, Sher, essentially it will be just the two of you, the greatest exponent of Sherlock Holmes on the stage, the world's greatest collector his audience. What a story. And you might be able to work in the Mystery of the Sherlock Holmes Manuscript you've been telling me about as well, quote a few passages, say how it came into your hands.'

'I couldn't possibly do that. The manuscript doesn't belong to me.'

'Okay, but you could still mention it. You'll write the article?'

'I suppose so. I don't see that I should be breaking any promise to Waymark, because I haven't made one.'

This unexpectedly ready compliance induced caution in Desmond. 'It might be an interview. Harry Morley's dead keen for you to write an article, but the man up there may not go along with that.'

'The man up there?'

'The editor.'

'Oh yes. I don't want words put into my mouth, I won't accept that.'

'Leave all that side of it to me, Sher. You write it or say it the way you want, and if they ask for changes we'll fight the good fight. And win it.'

Desmond whistled as he put down the telephone. His contentment was brief. At six o'clock precisely Harry Morley rang back to say he was sorry, but the man up there wouldn't wear it, he thought readers had had enough of Castle Baskerville. Desmond told Sher the *Banner* had said no because of the editor's stupidity, but he was confident of selling the story to another paper.

He would have been upset if he could have been a fly on the wall at the discussion Morley had had with the man up there before telephoning.

'Nothing in it for us,' the editor said. 'Sherlock Holmes

was a boring old fart anyway, and readers don't want some has-been actor telling them about—'

'Agreed. But they're interested in the mystery of the Mogul. We've had more than one journo slung out trying to get a story and some pix.'

'So?'

'They've got to have some changes made to the lighting for the performance. The sparks are going down on Thursday. O'Malley told me so.'

'Who's O'Malley?'

'Haynes's agent.'

'He must be a stupid fart too.'

They both laughed.

When Val had finished telling Sher what a wonderful time he had had, how exciting it must have been to be in the middle of a gun battle, and how much she would have liked to meet Alvaro Higgins, a.k.a. Kozma, she settled down to read *The Kentish Manor Murders*. She read, as she did everything, with great concentration, chain-smoking as she turned the pages. Sher's teeth gripped a meerschaum which he had first smoked when playing Sherlock. Blue circles drifted to the ceiling.

'It's a fake,' she said when she had finished.

'What makes you so sure?'

'I dunno. I just have a general feeling it isn't right. Even the title sounds a bit modern to me. In Conan Doyle's day they called books and stories *A Study in Scarlet* or "The Mystery of the Second Stain" or "The Adventures of the Missing Gold Bars" or something like that. They didn't use a nasty word like "murder". Isn't that true?'

'It may be, I'm not sure. But in any case you can't say the thing's a forgery just because Conan Doyle hadn't used the word "murder" in a title before.'

'You really want to believe it's genuine, don't you? They picked the right person to play for a sucker.'

'I wish you wouldn't use such language. If there were any

phrases like "play for a sucker" in the manuscript, I shouldn't have taken it seriously for a moment. But let's assume you're right. The manuscript is a fraud. What can be the object of it?'

'Getting a quarter of a million pounds sounds like a pretty good object to me.'

'But then why try to approach Waymark through me? There must be a better way.'

'You think so? You told me Alvaro, I can't call him Higgins, tried to get in touch and had no luck. They keep a pretty tight hold on the Mogul. If it is the Mogul, not just an understudy.'

Sher put his fingertips together. Looking at him as she did now, in profile, smoke spiralling up from the pipe clamped between his teeth, Val thought he looked wonderfully like the Sidney Paget drawings of the great detective. 'You understand, don't you, that whether or not this manuscript is genuine, the fact of his interest makes it almost certain the man in Castle Baskerville is Waymark?'

'It's much more exciting to suppose he's an understudy.'

'Then what would be the reason for his interest?'

'I know, I know. Don't be such a bloody old stick in the mud, let a girl have a little fun. After all, you've been having all sorts of excitement, I just have to use my imagination. I think we should go and talk to Jerry.'

'Talk to Jerry,' he repeated in dismay. Val's cousin Jerry Brightside managed to embody in himself several aspects of modern life Sher found strongly distasteful. He was the founder of and chief shareholder in a firm known as CCC. One of those Cs stood for Computer, a word that in itself made Sher shiver. Phrases like 'efficiency quotient' and 'uncalibrated programmatic survey' dropped from Jerry's mouth continually, like little involuntary eructations. Jerry was very successful. He had a wife, two teenage sons who as he approvingly said were into computer language, three dogs, a house by the Thames near Sonning, and an apartment in the Swiss Alps used for family skiing holidays. All this made Jerry Brightside an objectionable character, and Val and Sher had named him the Great Computer Bore. Why should they want to talk to him, now or at any other time?

Val tapped the manuscript. 'You want to check whether this is genuine. Your opinion, my opinion, isn't of much importance. Jerry can check it scientifically.'

'How would he do that?'

'You'd have to ask him, but I know it's the kind of thing that can be done, they add up the number of times the word "the" is used, something like that. People say it's the only reliable approach.'

He refrained from asking 'what people', and said he supposed there might be something in it.

'Of course there is. And you know Jerry, he'd do anything for me.' It was true that Jerry, although a year or two younger than Val, always treated her with a flirtatiousness Sher found peculiarly irritating.

'All right, you'd better see him. I want to show the manuscript to Peregrine.'

'But he's retired.'

'That means he'll have all the more time to look at it. And he's a genuine scientist, not a machine that spews out bits of paper.'

Peregrine Prout had been adviser to half a dozen different police forces on the authenticity of documents. He had a special interest in the forgery of handwriting.

'He's very crankish.'

'Never mind, he really is an expert.'

'And the last I heard he was being looked after by two women and still drinking himself to death.'

'I don't know where you hear such things,' he said admiringly. 'But however he's living and whoever it's with, he still knows more about genuine and false documents than anybody else in Britain.'

*　　*　　*

'Looking lovelier than ever if I may say so.' Jerry Brightside held Val's hand tightly for a moment, then released it with a reassuring pat.

'Never any harm in saying things like that, especially if they're obviously untrue. This is the problem we hope you can solve for us, the manuscript we talked about on the phone.' She produced a copy of *The Kentish Manor Murders*. Jerry gave it a cursory glance, then sat down behind his desk. He was a small man, and it was a large desk. Only head and shoulders were visible above it. His manner was businesslike.

'You want CCC to tell you whether this is a genuine Conan Doyle manuscript. Let me say at once that's something we can do, and quickly. In hours. Perhaps even in minutes.'

'Wonderful.'

'*But.*' An admonitory finger appeared above the desk top. 'To programme it we need information from you. You tell us what you want, and Billy Boy will produce the results, do I make myself clear?'

'No. Who's Billy Boy?'

'That's the name of the little fellow who'll be working for you.' Jerry's eyes gleamed, he put hands on desk, leant over it in his enthusiasm. 'A client gets results he doesn't expect and blames the computer, instead he should blame the information fed into it. *Billy Boy is never wrong*, do you read me? Give him the right facts, the relevant materials, he gives you the answers. But suppose you don't give him the facts, don't give him all of them? You're looking for a murderer, you read me? And you give Billy Boy details of the suspects, you want to know which of them is left-handed, blue-eyed, over six feet tall, he tells you. But you forget to tell him you know the killer has six fingers on his left hand, well, *you* don't tell Billy Boy he's not going to tell *you*. Don't think it, Val, not even a lovely lady like you. He won't do it, so just don't expect it.' Jerry shook his head vigorously. 'Be reasonable.'

Val took out a packet of cigarettes. Jerry continued to shake his head. 'Not in here, I'm afraid.'

'The smoke's not good for Billy Boy?'

'You're a great kidder, Val, we both know that, but it's true. Not only Billy Boy, all our machines are smoke-susceptible. It's a problem we're working on. In the meantime—' He pointed at the 'No Smoking' sign on the wall.

'You're saying that if we don't feed in the right information we shan't get the right answers. What sort of information?'

'How can *I* tell *you*?' Jerry laughed. 'I don't know, Billy Boy doesn't know, you need to ask Sherlock himself. By the way, how is old Sher? The word I hear is Sherlock Holmes is just about played out, needs to get up to date, but that's easier said than done. You couldn't expect him to play what's his name, James Bond, could you?'

'Just for your information James Bond is hardly more up to date, as you call it, than Sherlock Holmes. And Sher has just given his readings from the works in Copenhagen. To a packed house.'

'Is that so? Glad to hear there's life in the old dog yet. But you wanted to know the kind of thing you should give Billy Boy. It has to be something he can get his teeth into, make comparisons. How many times Sherlock said "Elementary, my dear Watson", that kind of thing.'

'Easy. He never said it.'

'Val, you are not reading me.' Jerry got up, walked round the room ticking off points. 'First, Billy Boy needs a lot of material for comparison. You could make it a word check – choose certain words that are special to these stories, check how often they appear in other stories compared to this one. Then do the same thing with names, places, occupations, particular typical phrases, there are some which must be special to Sherlock Holmes stories. Say you feed in one of these, Billy Boy tells you it has a median of thirty appearances in every volume and only appears once in this manuscript, maybe you're on to something, though of course Billy Boy would never make a judgement on just one sample and I'm no expert, far from it. If old Sher can come up with the fodder Billy Boy will consume it and produce the goods.'

'But getting together material of that sort might take days, even weeks.'

'Could very well be. It has to be carefully chosen.'

'I thought if I gave you this, you might be able to tell me something.'

Jerry laughed heartily. 'Even Andy and young Jerry would know better than that. I tell you, Val, some of the things those kids have rigged up on their own frighten me.'

'If they frighten you they'd probably scare me to death. Thank you, Jerry, we've been wasting each other's time.'

'It's no go Billy Boy the computer. He can give you an answer in minutes providing you do six months' work first.'

'I never had any faith in such new-fangled devices.' Sher spoke with satisfaction. 'I've spoken on the telephone to Perry, and sent him a copy of the manuscript. I'm going to see him this evening.'

'How did he sound?'

'Delighted to help. I think he's pleased to have something to do. Oh, I see what you mean, he sounded perfectly sober. Will you come with me?'

'Can't. There's a meeting of the Antique Dealers' Association I ought to attend, all about the wickedness of auction rings and what we shan't do to stop them. But in any case Perry after Jerry would be more than I could bear in a single day.'

Peregrine Prout lived in Kentish Town, in what had been a workman's cottage and was now part of a gentrified street where the front doors had all been newly and brightly painted. Or all except one. Perry's door was a dingy black, the paint peeling in places. The house number was 21, but the metal 1 had dropped off. The door was opened by a short dark woman in her thirties.

Sher introduced himself. 'How do you do?'

'If you're interested I do bloody awful.' She led the way down a passage, opened a door.

'My dear fellow, what a pleasure to see you. It's been too long.' Peregrine rose with difficulty from an armchair. He was in his late sixties, a bulky man who had run to fat, so that an outer layer of flesh had thickened the body Sher remembered, and changed the face so that there now seemed too much of it, the nose enlarged and reddened, the wobbly mouth bigger than it had been. He wore an old dressing gown and carpet slippers. 'Erica, it would be delightful if we could have a little snack.'

'Balls.' Erica closed the door with some force.

'Women are a problem, don't you think? Perhaps not, do you still have the same delightful wife? You do, yes, very clever of you. To me they have always presented an insoluble problem. One can't do without them, I find, yet at the same time they are the most eccentric creatures. You may have noticed some tension in Erica, an air of strain? I thought so, yes, you are perceptive, you noticed she was making a *to-do*. Can you believe the reason is that another old friend of mine named Lucinda has turned up after several years, and is staying here? Women do turn up, don't you find? They go away and then turn up again, and you really don't know where you are. You might have thought Erica would be pleased that the burden of looking after me was to be shared, but that isn't the case. Really I've given up trying to fathom women, they're beyond me.'

While saying this Perry had been pottering about, pouring whisky into two glasses, adding water, and picking up one or two among a pile of books on a large table in the middle of the room, opening them, chuckling or shaking his head, and replacing them. Among the books and papers Sher saw his xerox copy of *The Kentish Manor Murders*.

'Sit, sit, my dear fellow. Oh, forgive me.' The two other chairs in the room were piled high with books. Perry lifted one, tipped the books on the floor, perfunctorily dusted the seat with a dirty handkerchief. Sher sat down. 'A pretty little problem you've set me.' He took from the table the manuscript and several volumes, *The Art of Calligraphic Forgery* and *The Examination of Suspect Documents* among them. 'And you have cunningly provided a stumbling block by giving me not the original but a copy. If I had the original I could check the paper, the age and quality of the ink.'

'I'm sorry, that was not possible. I haven't seen the original myself.'

'Quite, quite, no need for apology, we shall reach a conclusion never fear, I merely point out the obstacles placed in my path.' He took a longish draught. 'Fortunately I have been able to obtain a work which provides an adequate sample of Sir Arthur Conan Doyle's calligraphy, a short story reproduced in manuscript. On a superficial comparison the writing in the story appears identical with your manuscript. But a superficial likeness only, my friend. Have you considered the line quality, did you make a proper examination of the pen-lifts?'

At this moment Sher realised, with a sinking heart, that Peregrine Prout was drunk. His articulation was perfect, what he said sounded and perhaps was sensible, but he was like a machine that has been wound up and will go through its performance regardless of questions or interruptions. So now, when he said he did not know what was meant by line quality and pen-lifts, he could not be sure that Perry heard him.

'The line quality in good handwriting shows few abrupt changes in curvature, and any variations are smooth and continuous. The Conan Doyle short story has the excellent line quality of a practised writer. Your manuscript however is an attempt to imitate the natural flow, so that in some places quite naturally there is lumpiness. Come here, let me show you. Look at that. D'you see, eh, d'you see?'

Sher could not truthfully say he did see. The two specimens of handwriting looked much the same to him. He asked about pen-lifts.

'Pen-lifts, yes, very good point, glad you brought it up.' Did he think he was addressing a class? 'You find them in almost all handwriting forgeries. The writer pauses, wonders if he's done it perfectly, and the result with a fountain pen or old-fashioned nib, anything except one of those confounded ballpoints, is a thickening of the letter. I've ringed round a few of 'em, look for yourself.' Sher looked at the letters ringed round. The thickening was certainly present, but could it not also be found in some letters in the short story? He pointed out what seemed such letters. Perry banged his glass on the table.

'Not the same thing at all. It's a matter of structure, master patterns, fluency and rhythm. I don't wish to seem harsh, my dear sir, but are you aware of the law of natural rhythm, and the theory of limited variation? I thought not. May I suggest, then, that you are hardly qualified to express an informed opinion?' He took another swig of whisky, emptied the tumbler and immediately refilled it.

'Perry, this is Sher. I'm not arguing with you, I know I don't have what you call an informed opinion. I just want to try to see those differences for myself.'

'Sher, my dear fellow, I forgot myself for a moment. Forgive me. Where is that snack, I'm devilish hungry.'

As though on a signal the door opened. Erica entered, made a space on the table, put down a plate, said, 'Ham sandwiches,' went out again.

Peregrine rubbed his hands. 'Ham sandwiches, just the job. Fall to, young Haynes, and tell me news of the world of grease paint and pretence.'

Sher ate a sandwich, said he had been playing Sherlock in Copenhagen, then returned to the manuscript. 'It's your opinion that this is a forgery.'

Perry raised a fat hand. 'I do so solemnly swear.'

'Supposing it came to a court case, would you be prepared to give evidence?'

Perry paused, glass halfway to mouth. 'Ah, there's the rub, as you prancers on the boards might say.' He looked down at the plate of sandwiches, shook his head. 'It is one thing, my young Sherlockian investigator, for me to tell you within these four walls that the pieces of paper you have shown me are worthless, an attempt no doubt to perpetrate some fraud, quite another matter to prove such a thing in court. Juries, as I have good reason to know, are sceptical people, reluctant to accept what an expert like myself knows to be true. Will you have another sandwich? I find myself after all not to be hungry.'

Sher said no to the sandwich. 'You mean—'

'I have given you an expert's opinion. And it is correct, make no doubt about that. But for the rest—' He paused, looked at the almost empty whisky bottle. '—I must ask you to forgive me, feel extraordinarily tired. Very good of you to pay an old man a visit, much appreciated, give my regards to. . . ' He pressed Sher's hand warmly, blundered towards the door, opened it. Erica was revealed on the other side, glaring at them. She said to Perry, 'You're blind drunk.'

'Nothing of the kind,' Peregrine Prout said with perfect clarity. 'A nap, snooze, forty winks, all that's needed.' He turned back to Sher, repeated the handshake. 'Most extraordinarily kind of you to look in.' A little unsteadily he approached the narrow stairs.

'You're killing yourself, you know that?' Erica shrieked. 'Bloody drinking yourself to death.'

Perry was now on the stairs. He made the mistake of trying to turn round, swayed against a banister, sat down heavily. 'And why not?'

Erica muttered something, put an arm round him, and half-lifted, half-dragged him up the rest of the flight. At the top they disappeared into what was no doubt a bedroom, a door closed. Sher let himself out.

Anna Ridley knew Paul's tastes. The meal she cooked for him, grilled fish followed by a sorbet, was simple and delicate, the flowery Moselle suitably unsubstantial. Afterwards they listened to a recording of *The Magic Flute* without speaking to each other. When it was over he sighed.

'Your genius, Anna, is that you knew instinctively this was an evening for grilled fish and Mozart.'

'Not roast beef and Wagner, you mean? Put it down to luck.'

'I do nothing of the kind. We're tuned to each other, you and I. It's a pity—'

'No use going on about that. Anyway, what you mean is that I remember there are certain things you're not supposed to eat, and don't give them to you. And when you say we're tuned to each other, what you mean is I'm tuned to you. I haven't noticed you worrying about tuning in to me.'

'I don't ask questions about who else you see. It's not that I'm uninterested, just I don't think you'd like it.'

'You're right about that.'

'And I know, or I can guess, when you don't want to make love. Like this evening.'

'Right again.' She paused, spoke slowly. 'I see a lot of different people around, not just journos and the rag trade. It's said there's some bother coming down at your prison. What kind I don't know.'

'And you don't know when?'

'No, I haven't got any details.'

'Whatever it is, the lads can look after it.'

'There's something lacking in you, Paul,' she said. 'You're intelligent, you're tough and you're generous. But you're careless. It's not exactly that you trust people too much, you're too confident that you're brighter than they are. Maybe that's right, but being so sure about it makes you less so. Sometimes you're so clever you're stupid.'

'Many thanks.'

'I'm telling you now, watch your back. It might be a good idea to go back to the prison shades tomorrow.'

'I can't do that. I've got a conference at the office up here, details to sort out.'

'Suit yourself. You have been warned.'

11. Wednesday

Polly Flinders read: 'Molly slipped into Edward's warm embrace, felt an exquisite thrill as his lips gently brushed hers. Outside the beach house she could hear the sound of the waves on the beach, one beam of moonlight shone through the window. His kisses moved down to the lovely white column of her neck. "Take me, take me," she cried. "Edward, I am yours." '

The light was placed so that it shone on the page of *Molly's First Romance* and left the figure on the bed in darkness. 'Move your hand a little lower.' She did so.

'I'm no bloody good at it. Reading.'

'You don't understand. There is a sensuality beyond the commonplace, and it thrives on contrasts. The delicacy of your hand and the crudity of your voice as you read that foolish story, these make up a true erotic experience. Being good at one thing and not good at another, that is perfect. Continue your ministrations but combine them with the thoughts and feelings of sweet little Molly, my sweet little Polly.'

Five minutes later he told her to put down the book.

'Is it a good little Polly?'

'A very good little Polly who reads so beautifully badly, and does what she's told.'

'Does oo forgive oo's little Polly for being cross?'

The thin voice said, 'There is no need for baby talk. You know what I need, a good listener, somebody who can ease the misery of existence. I am not a fool, I know this is not agreeable for you. You do it for money.'

'Warry, darling, don't say that.'

'There is no call for endearments. You are easing the days of an old man, a living skeleton, and you have your reward. Perhaps I may give you more, I do whatever I wish. My friend Paul thinks he runs the Mogul's life. So he does, but only because the Mogul lets him. The Mogul does what he wishes, and if he wants to reward Polly Flinders he will.' She was going to thank him, but realised it would be better to stay silent. 'Now come and lie beside me, I have remembered an odd experience years ago with a man who claimed to be able to produce cloth, genuine hard-wearing cloth, by mixing coloured wood shavings and water. Understand that the Mogul knows your thoughts, lie beside me and listen. Do as you're told and you won't regret it.'

She did as she was told. One story about the Mogul's past led as always to another. It was almost an hour later when she said, 'Warry, can your little Polly say something?'

'Speak.'

'About Lavender. It wasn't what you said, you know, about sex. I think he's got some plan, he's in with people who want to cause you trouble.'

'What trouble?'

'I don't know, Warry, I swear I don't. If your Polly knew she'd tell you.'

He did not comment, told her to leave him.

Val took the call, came in to Sher laughing. 'He's a bit of a charmer, your Prime Minister.' She saw his baffled look. 'Wake up there, would I be talking about *that* Prime Minister? Paul Decker wants to talk to you.'

'That's certainly a wonderful wife you have.' Decker's

voice was rich, almost reverent. 'Not only wise but witty.'

'I think so too.'

'I'm up in London at the moment for my sins, but I called to say how much the Mogul is looking forward to your performance. You'll come down with Val on Thursday, won't you? I want to show you that Castle Baskerville has a reasonable cook and a good cellar, and I know the Mogul's longing for the chance of another talk. So be with us in time for dinner, please.' There was no change in his voice as he continued. 'I shall be very happy for you to show the Mogul the manuscript.' Sher was too much taken aback to reply. 'There isn't the slightest reason why he shouldn't buy it if the seller can offer proof it's authentic. But you'll tell him what you think about that, won't you? Please tell Val how much I look forward to seeing her again.'

How, he asked Val, could Decker have known about the manuscript? Then he exclaimed. 'Of course, the little man. The one I told you about in Copenhagen and Amsterdam. He was the man with the false beard and moustache at the Castle. But why should he have been following me?'

'Tailing is the modern word, I believe. As for the reason, I'll leave Sherlock Holmes to concentrate on it.'

He had done so for only a few minutes, to no effect, when the telephone rang. Whatever voice he had expected to hear, it was not that of Velda Mortensen.

'You remember me? Good. I am in London, and hope it will be possible to see you. I am here to speak for Alvaro.' He remembered what Peter had said about his wife and Alvaro Higgins. 'You have not changed your mind, you will be going to see Mr Waymark? Good, very good. Then I think we should talk. Is it possible you can come to see me? I am at the Mazeppa Cloisters, I tell you where it is.'

Sher had been thinking it would be a good idea to tell Desmond in person of his doubts about the projected newspaper article, and the Cloisters were no more than five minutes' walk from his office. He arranged to see Velda at eleven thirty, and to call on Desmond at midday.

Mazeppa Cloisters was a semi-circle of glass and concrete, its shape and size insulting the elegant early Victorian terrace beside it. He asked the gold-braided doorman what the Cloisters had replaced. The man stared at him.

'I dunno, sir. Houses, I suppose.'

'Whatever it may have been, something of human size and shape has been replaced by a monstrous growth.'

'If you say so, sir. Mrs Mortensen's seven-o-seven.' His gaze followed Sher towards the lift.

The ascent was soundless, the carpet along the corridor springy. As he approached 707 the door of the next room opened, a man started to come out, then stepped back again and the door closed. Sher had time to catch a glimpse of somebody tall and thin, wearing a grey suit. There was something familiar, although not recognisable, about the figure, as there may be about an acquaintance seen for the first time in years across a crowded room.

Velda Mortensen was wearing a black dress, perhaps as a mark of mourning, perhaps because it suited her. Her manner was businesslike.

'Would you like a drink? No, I agree, drinking before lunch is a bad idea. I told you I spoke for Alvaro, I am here to make the arrangements. If you like to sit, that chair is not as bad as it looks. Then we can talk.'

The chair, tubes with a piece of canvas between them, offered no visible means of support but was indeed surprisingly comfortable. Sher said he didn't know what there was to talk about.

'First of all the manuscript, you find it okay, yes?' Sher said he couldn't exactly say that, and told her of his attempts to check its authenticity. She listened impatiently. 'But you will take it with you and show it, okay? And you tell him the price. But you leave Alvaro out of it, he is just an agent, you tell Mr Waymark the manuscript was shown to you by Doctor Langer and Peter, which is the truth. Okay, agreed?'

'I can see no objection.'

'When you leave I give you a copy of the manuscript.'

'Another photocopy?'

'Of course. The original will be handed over at the meeting with Waymark.'

'You mean you want him to pay for it then? That would be impossible. It would be absurd for you to expect that he would make over the kind of sum Mr Higgins talked about when he has had no time for any proper examination. I couldn't consent to be a party to any such arrangement.' He stopped, because she was nodding.

'We understand, we agree. Mr Waymark must have time to examine it, consult his own experts and so on. This is how we do it. When the price is fixed we hand it over. We give him two weeks. After that he returns it, or he pays the price settled at the meeting. We show our good faith like that, agreed?'

'You're prepared to let Waymark keep the original, examine it, have the paper tested?' She nodded. Her eyes met his unwaveringly, two bright buttons. There was some purely sexual quality about her that pervaded the room like the scent of a cat on heat. When she leaned forward it seemed to him that he felt the warmth of her body. Her nails were blood red.

'So you will give Mr Waymark this photocopy, Mr Haynes, and come with him to the meeting place where we talk about the price. I cannot say where it will be, we must let you know that later. We have a friend in Castle Baskerville who will be in touch.'

It would be useless, he knew, to ask the friend's identity. He found himself saying, quite irrelevantly, 'Did you love Peter?'

'He never complained.'

'He believed that in Amsterdam you were meeting a lover. Was he right?'

'It is not your affair. I have known Alvaro a long time. Peter knew about it. What has this to do with our business?'

'Nothing, I suppose. I don't see why you want to involve me in this arrangement. If you give the actual manuscript to Waymark, let him keep it and check on it, I don't see he could ask for more. Since you have a friend in the Castle, why can't he make these arrangements?'

'I could say I am just a messenger and don't know, but that would not be true. I tell you one reason. If our friend is found passing this photocopy to Mr Waymark he would be in bad trouble. If it is you, what could they say? Mr Sheridan Haynes is so respectable, Sherlock Holmes is an Englishman, he will make sure there is fair play.'

He hardly believed a word of what she was saying, and saw no reason to tell her that Decker already knew he would be showing the manuscript to Waymark. He accepted the leather-bound volume she gave him, no mere folder this time. He opened it, and saw that each separate page had been put within a plastic folder. As he stood up to leave he remembered the man next door who had stepped back to avoid him, and asked if she knew her neighbour.

'My neighbour? I don't know what you mean.'

'In seven-o-six. He seemed anxious not to meet me. I have a feeling we'd met before.'

'I think it is your imagination. I do not know who is next door.'

He knew she was lying. On the way out he tapped at the door of 706, but there was no reply. The doorman watched suspiciously as he left.

Desmond often had an air of being just about to eat, or in the middle of eating. Now, as he hurriedly closed a drawer, Sher wondered whether his agent had been halfway through a pork pie. He explained that he had decided not to write the article they had talked about. Desmond, who had found that no other paper showed any interest in the idea, accepted this gracefully.

'It's up to you, old man. O'Malley proposes, Sher disposes.

I thought it was a cracking idea, but if you feel that sort of thing is beneath your dignity, so be it. I'll come up with something else, you slap it down, that way we'll both grow rich. I'm joking, of course. Everything set for the entry into Castle Baskerville, the great solo performance?'

'I think so. Decker rang this morning to say he expected to see Val and me on Thursday.'

'The PM himself, you move in exalted circles. I'll be thinking of you on Friday, Sher. And getting a paragraph or two into the media, I've never known an artiste yet who didn't benefit from getting into print.'

Outside Desmond's office Sher received a hearty slap on the back. He turned to see the red smiling face of Chauncey Rampton.

'Sher, old dear, good to see you, haven't met in ages. Got time for a pint? Of course you have.'

'But you were going in to see Desmond.'

'On spec, purely on spec, ten to one that dragon secretary would have said he was busy. Desmond's got no time for old chaps like me, nothing for you, he says, not much call for comics who're rising seventy and got two wooden legs.' Chauncey was in fact over seventy, and although neither of his legs was wooden some form of osteo-arthritis had attacked them so that he lurched along like a mechanical toy. Since his act had combined patter with falling about athletically around the stage while pursuing attractive girls, his variety career had ended, and he had turned to straight acting, appearing in a couple of the Sherlock Holmes TV stories. It was hard not to feel sorry for Chauncey, but the fact remained that he was a bore of the kind found only among old stage performers, with a memory for past triumphs and disasters that quickly glazed the eyes of those exposed to it. So now, nursing the pints of bitter he had ordered for them both, and settled comfortably into a corner, Chauncey burbled happily away about occasions and people most of whom Sher had never known. Chauncey went back a long way, and his references to figures who were barely names to Sher were interspersed with occasional, slightly condescending references to those who appeared on cinema or TV screens. 'Larry, Ralph, great actors they were my dear, of course *great* actors, but could they perform in front of these cameras, ordered to do this, stand there, make sure they held a two shot? No no, my dear, they needed the wooden O, the boards to stand and stamp on. . . '

Sher saw with dismay that Chauncey's glass was still half-full. It would be grossly impolite to leave without ordering a refill. 'Drink up,' he said hollowly.

'I'm in no hurry.' Chauncey glared at him. It would be too cruel to say he was busy, had to go. He did his best to absent himself from the flux of reminiscence about Bongo and Willy, the Trilby Sisters, Que Voulez-Vous from Over the Water, Little Miss Muffet and others, when he heard Chauncey say, or rather repeat, 'The Great Panjandrum.'

'What's that?'

'I said the Great Panjandrum was always like that, stand-offish.'

'But what did you say happened?'

'My dear, if you'd only *listen*. I was having a pint in the Green Room, that very pleasant little dive just off Knightsbridge, and perhaps it wasn't just one but two or three, and I thought Chauncey my boy you're getting just a leetle bit tiddley, time to get back to the little woman, and I left and there under a street lamp I saw the Great Panjandrum, clear as I see you now. So I said to him, hallo Jonty my dear, you remember that was his rather preposterous name, Jonty Johnson, and he looked *through* me as if I wasn't there, and walked straight on. I know we'd not seen each other for, oh, ten years at least, but we'd been on the same bill very often, never at the top I grant you, but with quite respectable spots, thank you very much.'

'The Great Panjandrum,' Sher repeated wonderingly. 'Jonty Johnson.'

'As ever was. I can assure you there was no mistake, Jonty

was always what you might call cadaverous and now is more so, but I could never be mistaken about him, and I ask you is that any way to treat an old friend?'

Sher was not listening. He knew now why the man who emerged from 706 had seemed familiar. But why should Jonty Johnson, alias the Great Panjandrum, a man he knew slightly, have avoided him as well as Chauncey? He brooded on the problem during the next twenty minutes, in which he dutifully bought Chauncey a second pint and heard more theatrical tales of long ago, but did not come up with a reasonable answer.

Brian the Gate Officer was off duty, and Eric Malby was in the Gate House when the van arrived. He rang Hurst and then returned to the two men.

'You're not due until tomorrow.'

'They didn't call you?' the senior of the two asked incredulously. He wore jeans and a blouson. 'You're down to Plymouth today, Sid, they said, you can fit in this little job on Dartmoor, just a matter of fixing a couple of Starlette fresnels. You brought the Starlettes, Joe?'

Joe, a sharp-faced young man in his early twenties, nodded. 'And some profiles too, just in case, 263s and 264s.'

'I dunno,' Malby said. 'Should be Thursday by rights.'

'Now look, my friend,' the man with the blouson said, 'it's today or it doesn't happen. All this bother is down to the little tart in the office, don't worry, she says, I'll look after it, then she's too lazy to pick up the phone. But it has to be today, tomorrow we're up in Leeds.'

'I s'pose it's all right, but I got to give you a body check.'

'You'd think we were IRA,' Joe grumbled. The other man frowned at him. The body check completed Eric looked in the van, saw nothing but lighting equipment, cable, and stands for the lights, and said they should drive over to the Castle entrance where they would be met. They found a man wearing a uniform with a flash that said 'General Duties', who said he would give them a hand with the equipment.

'Don't worry, mate, you keep your health and strength,' Sid said. 'I got the stuff we'll need, and Joe'll bring the rest of the gear. You just lead on, Macduff.' They were led into the cinema where Sid looked round critically, then consulted his notes.

'Not what you'd call an ideal set-up. He's giving this show for just one person, right? Sounds as if somebody's missing a few of his marbles.'

'He's what they call a recluse,' General Duties said. 'Doesn't like seeing people.'

'Is that right? I like company myself, but it takes all sorts. You know, Joe, I believe you were right, I reckon we'll need one of those 263s, maybe two. You bring them in?'

'They're in the van.'

'Let's have 'em then, start trying a set-up.' Joe made for the door.

'Hang on a minute,' General Duties said. He had been told to stay around with the electricians. 'I'll get it for you.'

'No use, mate, would you know a 263 if it came up and spoke to you?'

'I'll come with you then. You might get lost, this place is a maze.'

'Suit yourself.'

They went out together. Sid, whose other name was Cassidy, moved quickly to get his Canon out of the Starlette. He would have perhaps ten minutes while Joe fumbled about in the van, and the idea was to take what pictures he could in that time, then return to the cinema, apparently complete the work, and leave. If it was possible to get any shots of Waymark that would be a big plus, though he'd been told not to risk doing so if it was likely to raise the alarm.

With the Canon out Cassidy began taking pictures. First the room itself, cinema to be used as theatre, then out into the corridor and along to the gallery above the great hall. He got excellent shots of the hall, stained glass windows, stags' heads on walls, entrance. He looked at his watch, saw only four minutes had gone. Back to the cinema, or should he chance going through the door that he knew led into Waymark's rooms? He chanced it.

Inside he was surprised by the near-darkness, knocked against a table, stopped. Nobody seemed to have heard him. The door ahead probably led to Waymark's living room. If he could get in there just for a minute he would get a unique picture. He moved towards the door, softly, silently.

Then it opened, and a tall figure was framed in it. Waymark? He snapped a couple of shots just in case, then the figure said, 'Hey, you man, what you doin'?' and he knew it was not Waymark, turned and ran. Behind him he heard a whistle. He reached the gallery, took the great staircase two stairs at a time and had almost reached the front door when a tackle from behind brought him jarringly to the ground. He was punched and kicked, the camera was taken, dropped to the floor, stamped on. Then he was frog-marched to the van where he found Joe, who had successfully delayed things by pretending to look for a flood which he had said they were sure to need.

'I think you've broken a rib,' Sid said to the young man wearing a frilled shirt who had attacked him most savagely.

'Next time we'll be using a shotgun,' Jimmy said. 'Why can't you bastards leave an old man alone?' He went with them to the outer gate and made sure they were away. Then he reported to Hurst, and said no harm had been done.

'A man in the Mogul's suite taking pictures,' Hurst said incredulously. 'How did it happen? Why was the camera not discovered? Who was at the Gate House?'

'There was a proper body check,' Jimmy said defensively. 'Nothing showed up. They must have had the camera hidden, the van was full of clobber.'

'The van was not properly searched?' Hurst looked over his half-moon glasses at Jimmy. 'I see it was not. Who was in charge at the Gate House?'

'Watson was at tea break or something. Eric Malby was standing in.'

'Send him to me.' Jimmy began to protest, to say that any decision about what should be done ought to wait until the PM returned, and that the real problem was how the pressmen had known enough to come a day before the genuine electricians were due.

'Somebody opened his mouth,' Hurst said succinctly. 'Those are matters for me. Malby should have searched the van properly, you know that perfectly well. Send him to me, please. Now.'

An hour later Malby had left Castle Baskerville.

12. Thursday and Friday

Decker returned to Castle Baskerville just before midday, glad as always to get back to what he thought of as his personal realm. It was true that he ruled it as Regent rather than as King, but still his control was absolute. His serenity was soon disturbed, first by Jimmy who told him of the attempt to take pictures and of Malby's dismissal. Then came Hurst, with a different slant on the same story. Jimmy had taken the view that the dismissal was hasty. When Decker said this, Hurst's lips were pressed even more tightly than usual.

'As you know, there had been complaints about him before.'

'Made by Watson, the Gate Officer. Why was he not on duty?'

'He was at tea break. I should take some part of the blame, since I could have called the *Banner* to check the men's credentials, but their visit was expected, and the explanation for it being on Wednesday rather than today seemed reasonable. But nothing can excuse Malby's failure to check the van and their equipment properly. The lighting technicians, the genuine ones, came early this morning. The work is done, everything is ready. Perhaps it should be made clear to Jimmy that I am responsible for administration here.'

Decker nodded. He was gathering papers together for a visit to the Mogul when Doctor Prettyman appeared.

'Dave, hallo. How was the wheel of fortune?'

The doctor's smile was like a wince. 'I return poorer than I left, much poorer. But never mind that, there is something you should know. Polly Flinders came to me this morning with a tale about Lavender. She thinks he's using some drug on the Mogul that will place him under Lavender's influence.'

Decker stared at him. 'Is it likely?'

'It's possible. He would be in a position to do it. I've examined the Mogul. He's in a highly nervous state. Apparently the girl had been hinting things to him, but he trusts Lavender.'

'There were no positive indications that he'd been drugged?'

The doctor's smile became more tortured. 'Almost all patients under constant medication take drugs. We give the Mogul drugs every day.'

'I never liked that little bitch,' Decker said without heat. 'I thought she was Lavender's girl friend, perhaps they've fallen out. Did she say anything specific?'

'She said Lavender had boasted to her that he'd soon have the Mogul eating out of his hand, doing anything he said, signing anything he wanted. She thought she ought to speak to somebody, you weren't here, I'm the Mogul's doctor.'

'She's just making trouble for Lavender.' The doctor stroked his lantern jaw. 'You don't mean to say you think there's something in it?'

'There might be.'

'Have you talked to Lavender? You haven't? I think we should.'

'No point in it. We should just be warning him if he's up to something, make him angry if he isn't. Either we leave it alone or search his room.' Decker was startled. 'I know you don't trust Polly Flinders, but you didn't talk to her this morning. I don't know if she was right, but she meant what she said, no doubt about it.'

They found the Mogul in his darkened bedroom, fretful and anxious, his thin voice pitched high.

'Is this what I pay for, both of you away at the same time? I won't have it, I tell you, I'm just not prepared to tolerate. . . ' He seemed to lose the thread of what he was saying, subsided into only partly audible grumbling. Decker switched on the light used by Polly for reading and said it was all right now, they were back. The Mogul turned his face to the wall. Lavender appeared in the doorway, asked if he could help.

Prettyman said, 'I want to talk to you, Lavender. Not here, in your apartment.'

Left alone with the Mogul, Decker tried to interest him in the papers he had brought along, without success. To anything he said the reply was petulant. 'I'm not prepared to consider that now. . . I don't agree. . . I *don't* want to look at the papers and I'm *not* going to sign them.'

It was like talking to a fractious child. Decker said, 'I'm sorry you're so unwell. Mr and Mrs Haynes are coming down today, and he's due to give his performance tomorrow. Perhaps I'd better call and try to postpone it. That would be a pity.'

There was silence. Then the man in the bed said pleadingly, 'Paul, I have had such a horrible time, I am upset. That girl has been saying things and they upset me. I must *not* be upset.'

'Of course you mustn't. Perhaps she'd better go.' He regretted these last words as soon as they were spoken, and sure enough the Mogul cried out that he could not be left without a listener. 'We'll get you another listener. A better one.'

'Yes yes, she was not really satisfactory. I can't remember a really satisfactory listener since. . . I can't remember. Paul, I must pull myself together, mustn't I? I shall put on my dressing gown and watch one of Mr Haynes's films. That will be a tonic, the best a man can have. Perhaps I shall get dressed, I received him last time in my dressing gown, that wasn't right. Ask Lavender to come and help me. Oh oh, what's that?'

He put his hands over his ears. There was the sound of raised voices, Prettyman's and Lavender's, from the next room. Decker told the Mogul not to worry, said he would be back in a moment, and went in. Lavender was sitting on his bed, and he looked now from one to the other of them. Prettyman held out two white envelopes. Decker asked what they contained.

'This one's a drug called Arcantil, used for treating epileptics. The effect is tranquillising, but it also makes the patient very compliant, ready to do anything he's told if it seems reasonable and possible. He wouldn't jump off a cliff if you told him to after he'd taken a couple of these, but he would sign a cheque. I found them in the bathroom cupboard.'

'They're not mine, I tell you. They been planted on me.'

'And the other envelope?'

'Cocaine. In a drawer of his bedside table. And a syringe.'

'It's just lies,' Lavender said. He went to a window, pulled aside the curtain, rolled up his sleeves. 'You see anything? I don't do drugs, I tell you, that bitch planted 'em on me, couple nights ago she came across, stayed here a while, nice as pie and two weeks before that she wouldn't look at me. She came over just to plant stuff.'

'Why would she do that?'

'How the hell do I know?' Lavender shouted. 'I'm just telling you I don't do drugs, never have.'

'Keep your voice down,' Paul Decker said, too late. The skeletal figure of the Mogul appeared in the doorway, dark glasses covering his eyes. His head turned from one to the other of them.

'Just a little problem,' Decker said. 'Has Lavender here

asked you to sign any papers or documents lately? Or do anything special for him? Anything at all?'

'I don't know what you're talking about. I cannot be worried about such things. If you'd not both been away this would not have happened.'

'What do you mean? What happened?'

'How do I know? *Something* must have happened or you wouldn't be shouting. I am going back to my room, I can't endure it.'

When he had gone Decker looked at the doctor. Prettyman's mouth was turned down in a sneer. He advanced on the nurse, who retreated.

'You get well paid here, three times what you'd get in private nursing, but you got a habit and the money wasn't enough, say it.' Lavender shook his head. 'Why else did you have the Arcantil, maybe you're epileptic, just tell us. You're through here, Lavender, you can pack your stuff and go.'

Decker said, 'Dave.' Prettyman turned a furious face on him.

'You run everything here, you're the PM, make the decisions, but this is my patient. Are you telling me I've got to say yes to him having a nurse who does drugs and has this Arcantil here he can't explain? Okay, I accept part of it is down to me, I shoulda kept my eyes open wider, but now they've been opened for me don't tell me I got to shut them again. I want him out. Now.'

Decker nodded. 'All right. Lavender, it has to be the way Doctor Prettyman says. Unless you can come up with an explanation.'

The nurse said sullenly, 'What would be the point? I already told you what happened, but you don't believe it. The stuff was planted on me, there's only one person coulda planted it, and that's Polly.'

'I heard maybe you'd broken up, but why would she do that?' Decker said earnestly, 'I'd really like you to tell me.'

'You better ask her, not me. Could be something to do

with that Gate Officer Watson, the smartypants she's been playing around with.'

Prettyman shook his head. Decker spoke gently. 'I'm afraid I can't accept that. You'd better leave today. Go and see Mr Hurst. I'll speak to him and see you get compensation as long as you sign the usual forms.' Every employee leaving voluntarily or being dismissed was asked to sign a form saying he or she would not grant interviews to the press for a period of two years. If they broke the agreement they lost the handsome compensation.

Afterwards they went to see the Mogul. The doctor examined him, and said he was in reasonable shape. Decker broke the news about the nurse's departure, and told him what had been happening in London. The Mogul's reactions were always unpredictable. Now he said that he'd got sick of having a black nurse, and was sick of Polly too. Perhaps it might be possible to get a young nurse, female, who would also be a listener? That might be possible, Prettyman said, and in the meantime he would come across and stay in Lavender's rooms himself. What the Mogul really wanted to talk about, however, was Sheridan Haynes's visit. Was everything ready, would Paul bring him over the moment he arrived, and make sure he had everything he wanted.

'I know why you've arranged it, as a little treat for me,' he said to Decker. 'A little bit of what he wants will keep him happy, he won't interfere or step out of line. Correct?' He looked from one face to the other, but the Prime Minister's smile remained easy, and Prettyman's expression of lantern-jawed gloom did not change. 'And you may be right. But Warren Waymark knows what's going on, always did, nobody was ever too smart for him. Don't you forget that. Warren Waymark's top dog, what he says goes. Know who I said that to, years ago? Dave Dubinsky of the Garment Workers, and Dave said to me. . . '

It was twenty minutes before they got away, Decker to

talk to Hurst about Lavender's dismissal, Prettyman to move over into Lavender's apartment.

Sher and Val arrived in the late afternoon. This time there was no trouble at the gate, and they were warmly greeted by the curly-haired Gate Officer.

'Where's Grumpy?' Val asked. He looked baffled. 'Eric or little by little, who was so pleased to see us last time.'

'Gone. He gave everybody the same warm welcome, and was slack with it. Yesterday he let in some news photographers posing as electricians come to fix things up for you, didn't check to see if they had cameras, so goodbye Eric. We can get along without him.' In reply to Sher's question he said that yes, the genuine articles had been along that morning, and he understood everything was fixed up. Val asked whether Mr Waymark was looking forward to the show. He gave her a brilliant smile, rolled his eyes.

'No use asking me. I hear a lot about the Mogul but I've never set eyes on him. He likes to be alone.' He lengthened the last word, Garbo fashion. 'I'll tell you who sees the great man. The PM of course, his doctor and nurse, a girl called Polly Flinders who comes over to sit with him and listen to him chuntering on about the great stuff he did thirty years ago. Oh yes, and Mr Hurst, our Gordon. He acts as stand-in when the PM's on leave. Five people, that's all, and it's five minus one now.' He told them about Lavender's departure.

They were in the Gate House, and Sher remembered seeing blonde hair through the window on their previous visit. 'You know Polly Flinders.'

The brilliant smile was turned on him. 'We've passed the time of day.'

After they had been escorted to the Castle Sher said, 'I wouldn't trust that young man.'

'Sherlockian intuition? Half the time it's right, the other half it's wrong, you might as well toss a coin. I thought he was nice. And the PM's nice too.'

The Prime Minister greeted Sher politely and Val with enthusiasm. He asked if their room was comfortable, and when they had said truthfully that it was, told them the programme.

'First I thought you might like to take a look at the set-up for tomorrow evening. Then we see the Mogul, who's been a bit temperamental, but is longing to talk to you again. Especially to Sher. I thought we might leave them to it, Val, and that you could look at the rest of the establishment. We're quite proud of the entertainment complex, and the residential quarters too, and I'd like you to see them if it wouldn't bore you. Then drinks over here, and dinner.'

'Not with Mr Waymark?' Val asked.

'No, he eats like a bird, and prefers to peck away on his own. A dinner party here is a bit of a problem.' His look was amused, quizzical. 'A place like this isn't good for marriages, or even unmarried couples. Dave Prettyman's been married more than once but it never stuck, Gordon's not married. Neither am I,' he said, anticipating a possible question. 'The lady took a good long look at Castle Baskerville and fled. So you can see a dinner party's liable to be top-heavy with men, and I'm afraid that's the way it'll be. I've asked our tennis coach Josh Taylor who's got a pleasant wife, and thrown in Polly Flinders just to make the balance a bit more even. Tomorrow you'll be free all day to sample the delights of Devon, though I'd like you to be back here by six.' Sher said they would pay a visit to his brother Brinsley. 'Fine. The reading's fixed for seven thirty, and you leave the following morning. Now I'll take you across to the Mogul. Ah, that's the great work,' he said at sight of the leather-bound volume given Sher by Velda Mortensen.

'Would you like to look at it?'

'What would be the point? My opinion would be worthless I'm afraid. But I told the Mogul you had a surprise for him, and he can't wait to see it.'

Sher said, 'The first chapter was stolen from me in

Copenhagen. It was taken by the man you had watching me, the one who wore a false beard when I met him here. Why was I being watched, Mr Decker?'

The Prime Minister looked taken aback, then laughed. 'I should have known it was impossible to deceive your sharp eye. He was doing a little job for me, and I asked him to make sure you didn't get into bad company.'

'And he stole the manuscript from my room.'

Arms spread wide in contrition Decker said, 'I gave him no such instructions, believe me. I couldn't be more apologetic. He's a private detective, and I've used him several times, but that was the last. I hope you'll count it to my credit that I told you on the telephone I knew about the manuscript. And in view of what happened I'm grateful to you for coming down.'

They traversed the same route as before to the Mogul's suite, but this time it was the doctor who met them, and not the black nurse. He gave a nod of greeting, and led them into the sitting room. Waymark rose from his armchair.

'Mr Haynes, I've been waiting impatiently to see you again, not only because of the performance tomorrow, but for the chance to see and talk to you. Those are rare pleasures in the life of a sick man.'

'Mrs Haynes is here too,' Decker said, but the Mogul gave her the most perfunctory greeting. He had put on a jacket and trousers, shirt and tie, and the effect was to accentuate his thinness, so that he looked like a scarecrow on which clothes had been hung. Perhaps the doctor was responsible for the formal dress, and for the drawing of the curtains so that light came through the darkened window glass. A strange scene, Sher thought, the skeletal figure in the armchair with his dark glasses and gloves, the brooding dark-jawed doctor who stood beside him like a protector or jailer, Val looking a little nervously at the two of them, and the bulky Prime Minister, the only person in the room who appeared altogether at ease.

There was a moment's silence, broken by Decker suggesting to Val that they should take a turn outside. When they had gone out through the French windows Prettyman said he would be next door if needed, and retreated to what had been Lavender's quarters. The Mogul, left alone with Sher, tapped with black-gloved fingers on the table beside him.

'Well, Mr Haynes? Well? Paul said you had a surprise for me, one I should enjoy. What is it?'

'First I must explain.' And Sher did so, telling how the manuscript had come to him at the luncheon with Doctor Langer, and the unsuccessful attempts to check its authenticity. The Mogul had seized the leather-bound book and was turning the pages eagerly, making a faint whistling sound under his breath. Was he listening, had he heard anything Sher said? He continued to turn the pages after Sher had finished speaking, pausing occasionally. Then he closed the book.

'What does this man Langer want for it?'

'As I said, he is not the owner. He is a professor of Sherlock Holmes studies at the University of Groningen.'

'Very good, very good. There should be such professors at every university. I should have heard of him before.'

'According to what I was told, the owner lives in Hungary.'

'Never mind. This Langer, or the man in Hungary, or whoever it is, what does he want for it?' Sher told him. 'I must have it.'

'And pay what they ask? That would be ridiculous.'

'What is ridiculous about it?'

'I'm sure it would fetch nothing like that at auction.'

A gloved finger pointed at him, the thin voice dropped to a whisper. 'Mr Haynes, there are not many things I want in this world, but I always get them. What you are showing me is unique, I have never seen or heard of anything like it. Neither have you, nor have all those fellows in Sherlock Holmes societies all over the world. I have money, and little to spend it on. Do you think it matters to me if I pay more than this unique manuscript would fetch at auction? If it went to auction I might lose it.'

There was something maddeningly complacent about the way he spoke. Sher found himself almost shouting. 'This is a photocopy, you've only glanced at it, you have no proof at all that it's genuine.'

'Nobody ever called Warren Waymark a fool in business matters, Mr Haynes. You tell me yourself that the owner or his agent will let me keep the original for two weeks before I make payment. There are experts in everything relating to Sherlock Holmes and over the years I have corresponded with many of them, although not with your Doctor Langer. If two weeks is not enough for them to provide me with their opinions, why then I shall still have the manuscript, and believe me I shan't pay for it unless I'm convinced it is genuine.' He wagged a finger at Sher, the dry voice was almost playful. 'Old as I am and invalid as I am, I still have a better head for business than a play actor.'

'I told you they insisted on talking about the details of the deal with you in person, and that they wanted me to be there.' Waymark had gone back to the leather-bound book and was reading it closely from the beginning, his lips moving. 'And I mentioned this friend they say they have here. He hasn't made himself known to you?' The head bent over the manuscript was shaken. 'How will you arrange it? I thought you never left the Castle.'

'Incorrect. I have left here, as you may have heard, when I wished to do so or thought it necessary. I am a voluntary hermit.'

Sher's irritation grew. 'Then why not have come to a public performance of my readings, why all this elaborate fandango about a special performance here? You say you're a voluntary hermit, but from what I've heard, when you have left it's not just been walking out, you make some sort of secret arrangement. That doesn't sound voluntary to me.'

He could not see the eyes behind the dark glasses, but the

thin lips were quivering. 'Mr Haynes, I don't permit people to speak to me like that. There are things I cannot tolerate, I won't have them, I shan't endure them. Questioning like yours makes me remember the things reporters used to ask me. I shall say *nothing more*, Mr Haynes, and if I am to remember my debt of gratitude to you there must be no more such questions, do you understand?'

His voice had risen to a piping shriek. Prettyman's head appeared round the door. 'Anything wrong?'

Waymark picked up the manuscript, rose a little unsteadily. 'Nothing, not in the mood for visitors. Or talking. I must retire, be alone.'

'Shall I tell Polly to come over?'

'I said I wanted to be *alone*,' Waymark screeched. He turned to Sher and said with obvious effort, 'I can't continue this conversation, must retire.' He went into his bedroom and closed the door.

'You say something to upset him? No need to worry, every so often he flies off the handle, happens over nothing. Only thing to do is wait till it's over, which is usually only a couple of hours. It's a fact he does have all kinds of things wrong with him, he's got this photophobia, digestion's not good, he suffers from eczema, but he imagines all of them are worse than they are. And he's afraid of crowds, hates publicity.' After what was for him a long speech Prettyman lapsed into silence.

'Will you give him a sedative?'

The doctor shook his head. 'Chances are he'll snap out of this in half an hour, forget the whole thing. Not very cheerful in here. Why don't you go over and join the PM and your wife?'

Sher met them coming back across the lawn. 'You should see what they've got over there,' Val said. 'Indoor tennis courts I'd love to play on, an Olympic-size pool, a gymnasium with so many bits of apparatus I couldn't recognise I thought it was a set from science fiction. It's fantastic, though I don't know it's a fantasy I should like to live in.' She noticed Sher's expression. 'What's up?'

'I'm afraid I upset Mr Waymark by one or two questions.'

Decker laughed when told what the questions had been. 'The Mogul's very touchy about all that. He's right to say he can leave here any time he wishes, Baskerville belongs to him, of course he can. And just occasionally he has this overwhelming urge to get away, but no sooner has he done it than he's terrified – you've heard about the time he landed up at Penzance and rang asking to be brought home again? For years now he's been incapable of coping with the outside world, and he's got a fear of the media that's almost pathological. Being cooped up here doesn't help, but nothing's going to change him now. He knows the way he wants things, and that's the way they have to be.'

'Should I go back and say I'm sorry?'

'No, leave him to simmer down. He's reached the stage when the distant past is much more real than what happens here and now. He goes on endlessly with his listeners about things that happened thirty or forty years ago, and they don't have to comment, he just talks. I don't know how they stick it. You said you'd like to play on our courts, Val. We can't fit you out with clothes, but we can supply a racquet and shoes, and I'm sure Josh would love to give you a game tomorrow morning.'

'It's a nice idea, but Sher's brother will be expecting us.'

'Tell me if you change your mind. And now it's almost drinks time, I'll lead the way back.'

The assurance of his manner was that of a landowner showing visitors round his estate, as Val said to Sher when they were in the privacy of their suite, the windows of which overlooked a small side lawn. 'And I suppose that really is his position. When he says Waymark's free to come and go as he pleases I believe him, don't you?'

She was at the dressing table. Sher said to her reflection, 'I thought your idea was that Waymark's dead.'

She made a face at him. 'It was Marty's idea really, not mine. And it still might be true.'

Sher shook his head. 'I'm convinced the man we've seen is Waymark. But there's something wrong. I don't know what it is, but I can feel it in the air the way we felt Hurricane Bobo approaching when we were in Florida, remember?' That had been when he was touring America with the readings. 'And something Waymark said reminded me of a question I should have asked, an obvious one. He said when I mentioned Langer, "I should have heard of him." ' He looked at the telephone beside their bed. 'I wonder if it's safe to use that?'

'You mean it might be bugged? You're dreaming.'

'Perhaps I am.' He picked up the receiver, dialled, and within a minute was asking Desmond O'Malley to find out whether there was a professor of Sherlock Holmes studies at Groningen, and what was his name. When Desmond protested Sher spoke sharply. 'You're always talking about all your contacts in other countries. Surely you have one in the Netherlands.'

'Of course, but—'

'Then talk to him. And quickly.'

When he put down the instrument Val made a soundless hand-clapping motion. 'My, I've never seen you so masterful.'

Sher ignored this. 'There's another thing. When I told Waymark the friend they're supposed to have here would get in touch with him to arrange a meeting, he paid almost no attention, hardly seemed to hear me. It was as if it came as no surprise to him. I wonder if Lavender could have been the friend, and if so whether that was why he was made to leave.'

'What is it you keep saying about theorising from insufficient information? Let's go down and join that lovely Paul. I'll tell you something. If he'd offered me marriage plus life at Castle Baskerville, I might not have said no.'

In the living room Jimmy was pouring champagne. Val was at once appropriated by Decker, and Sher found himself confronted by Polly Flinders, vivid in a red dress. 'Hi,' she said, using perhaps her invariable form of greeting. 'You're that actor's putting on a show for Warry, saw you the other day, didn't I? He's over the moon about it. He lets me call him Warry, not the Mogul like all the others, you know that? Are you famous?'

'Not famous. Just known for playing Sherlock Holmes.'

'Warry says you're famous. I said to him I never heard of Sheridan Haynes, goes to show I'm ignorant I s'pose. I used to be a stripper.'

'Don't you find it dull here?'

'Dull?' She rolled her eyes. 'Bored out of my mind is more like it. But the money's good and you got nothing to spend it on so you can't help saving, and I reckon a girl can spare a few months out of her life if she's getting paid for it. Mind you, when I was here first I had a little thing going with that black bloke Lavender, but I didn't like what he was doing to Warry.'

'What kind of thing was that?'

'Oh, stuff to get him under his thumb, you know, like so he'd do what Lavender said. Yes, thanks Jimmy, top me up.' When the young man had moved away she said, 'He fancies me, Jimmy I mean. You might think he was AC/DC with those frilled shirts and the way he acts as the PM's sort of butler, but I can tell you I've had to fight him off. I mean it's not as if I like him, not much anyway.'

Sher remembered the glimpse of her inside the Gate House. 'Perhaps you prefer Brian?'

The characteristic vacancy of her eyes was replaced by watchfulness. 'I wouldn't give him the time of day. If you'll excuse me, I need the little girl's room.'

She left the room as Prettyman entered it. The doctor paused in the doorway as if considering who should be favoured by his presence, then came over to Sher.

'You'll be glad to know the Mogul has quite recovered from his little paddy, asked me to say how excited he is about tomorrow evening. That's the nearest you'll get to an apology, I've never known him apologise for anything.'

'Have you left him alone? I thought somebody was meant to be on hand all the time?'

The doctor showed yellow teeth in a grin. 'I'm on permanent call over here, he only has to pick up the telephone and I'd be with him in not much more than a minute. And if I know him he might just do that.'

A burst of laughter came from the other side of the room, its source a group that contained Decker, Val, and two people Sher had never seen before. Decker said something, there was more laughter, and Sher said he seemed to be in fine form. Prettyman shook his head.

'He's not a well man.'

'Decker?' Sher said in surprise. 'You mean his diabetes? I thought that could always be controlled by insulin nowadays.'

'It can. Providing the patient does what he's told.'

'And Decker – the PM – doesn't?'

The doctor leaned forward, spoke into Sher's ear. 'You remember the tale about the Princess who ate only a few grains of rice each day, then feasted secretly at night. The PM is like that. There are stresses in his position, you can imagine them. He keeps control of himself in public, does it wonderfully, but when he's alone he eats cream cakes, drinks milky tea loaded with sugar, and God knows what else he gets up to.'

'You've spoken to him about it?'

'Of course. Sometimes he denies it, and then swears he won't touch another rich cake or eat any more sweets. But it's like an alcoholic swearing off drink, it doesn't last. And there's no Alcoholics Anonymous for diabetics.' He said to Jimmy, who had come round with the champagne bottle, 'Is the PM staying off the sugar and the sweet cakes and biscuits now, Jimmy?'

'Doesn't touch 'em,' Jimmy said with conviction, and

passed on. Prettyman shook his head gloomily, and said Jimmy was a faithful servant. A couple of minutes later they went in to dinner.

Decker sat at one end of the table, with Val on his right, and Pat Taylor, wife of the tennis professional, on the other side. Taylor was next to Val, with Polly Flinders on his right. Sher was placed between Mrs Taylor and Hurst, who had come in almost at the last moment. Prettyman was at the other end of the table.

Pat Taylor was thin and dark, with a nose that bent upwards at the tip. This, combined with the fact that she held her head upwards even when eating gave her a look of permanent disdain. When Sher said her husband must surely find rather a limited scope for teaching tennis at Castle Baskerville she bridled slightly.

'*Actually* that's only a small part of what Josh does, he's also in charge of swimming, golf and riding, so I can assure you his time's fully occupied. There's nothing like being up on a horse, nothing at all.' Her nostrils quivered slightly.

Sher said he supposed not, turned to Hurst, and asked whether there was much turnover of staff. Hurst looked at him carefully over the little half-moons, and said it varied.

'You seem to have had several losses lately.'

Hurst took a sip of the white wine in front of him. 'Two.'

'I know Mr Waymark doesn't like publicity. You must be worried about people selling their stories to a sensational newspaper.'

'They sign agreements.'

'But do they keep them?'

Hurst considered this at length, then said, 'Mostly.'

Sher caught the eye of Decker, who was looking at him with amusement. Now he said, 'You'll be lucky if you get twenty words at a time out of Gordon. Any secrets of Castle Baskerville are safe with him, aren't they, Gordon?'

'I hope so.' Hurst looked down at the tablecloth.

The food was simple, fillet of sole followed by a rack of

lamb. A moustachioed Italian wearing a chef's hat and apron carved it, and a waitress in a blue and white uniform served the vegetables. Decker ate and drank sparingly, and did not take the redcurrant jelly that came with the lamb. He had of course, Sher reflected, the doctor's eye on him.

His attention was distracted by Val crying out, 'There must be some, there *must* be.' Her neighbour Josh Taylor, red faced and jolly, said, 'There are not, I tell you. Just listen to this.' And he launched into some lines about cricket that Sher vaguely recognised, ending with

> 'And a ghostly batsman plays to the bowling of a ghost,
> And I look through my tears on a soundless-clapping host
>
> As the run-stealers flicker to and fro,
> To and fro:
> O my Hornby and my Barlow long ago!

And that's only one. I tell you there are books of 'em, whole books,' he ended triumphantly.

Polly Flinders said to Prettyman, 'What is it, what's he on about?' Prettyman shook his head. Val began to laugh as she saw Sher's look of mystification.

'They were both cricketers, Hornby and Barlow, played for Lancashire.'

'And England,' Taylor added.

'The poem's by Francis Thompson, is that right?'

'Quite right.' Taylor gazed at her fondly.

'Sherlock is baffled. What Mr Taylor says—'

'Make it Josh.' Taylor put a hand on Val's arm, removed it when he saw his wife's Medusa gaze on him.

'Josh says there are dozens of poems about cricket, whole books of them, but nothing about tennis, and he thinks it's a damned shame. I can't believe that's true.'

'Only one poem anybody knows.' Taylor held up a finger. 'John Betjeman, Joan Hunter Dunn. "What strenuous singles we played after tea, we in the tournament – you against me!"

But that's all, nothing else worth talking about. *There are no poems about tennis.*' He looked round defiantly, perhaps having drunk a glass too many. Nobody contradicted him.

He was not the only person to show the effect of drink. Polly, after downing a large brandy, began a tuneless rendering of 'Yellow Submarine'. Decker, who was talking to Val and Pat Taylor, seemed unaware of her voice, and it was Hurst who said in his unemphatic tone, 'That's enough, Polly.' She ignored him, and repeated 'We all live in a Yellow Submarine' a little louder.

Hurst said, 'Go to bed, Polly.'

She stopped, stared at him, then surprisingly said, 'Oh, all right.' She went over to Decker. 'Thank you, Mister Prime Minister, for giving a treat to one of the lower orders.'

'It was a mistake to think you would know how to behave,' Decker said. He glanced at Jimmy, who hovered beside the door.

'Sod you,' Polly replied, and went. Decker looked round, and said with his easy smile that there was no need to break up the party, but Hurst pleaded papers to look at and then the Taylors went, Josh telling Val it had been the greatest pleasure to find somebody interested in cricket and tennis. Sher took this as a cue to retire. Breakfast, Decker said, would be brought to their room at any time they wished. Eight thirty? Eight thirty it should be, Jimmy would see to it. Perhaps they would look in on him before going out in the morning.

'I call that an interesting evening,' Val said. 'That little sports instructor was such fun, spouting the cricket poems about ghostly batsmen and Hornby and Barlow and all that. Pity there aren't any tennis poems, perhaps we should write one together, d'you think?' She sat on the edge of the bed. 'I know what you're going to say, but I'm not drunk, just happy.'

The telephone rang. Sher answered it, heard Desmond's self-applauding voice. 'The things I do for the people I love,'

Desmond said. 'Instant service, miracles performed on the spot. Just listen. . . '

Sher listened. When he had put down the telephone he said, 'There's no Doctor Langer at the University of Groningen, and no Sherlock Holmes professor there. As I should have known.'

'And that means?'

'That means the manuscript is a fake, and very likely Langer was the man who faked it.'

'So?'

'So I shall tell Waymark in the morning, and that will be the end of it.'

She made a face. 'How disappointing. Oh well, let's go to bed.'

Sher went to bed, slept, dreamed. In his dreams Prettyman appeared, his jaws rotating steadily. He put hand to mouth and drew out long strings of white stuff, shaped them with black-gloved fingers so that they joined. I am making a net, he said, drawing more stuff from his mouth, a net for a tennis poem. Did you know the Mogul played tennis? Prettyman came very close, opened his mouth and revealed it as full of white stuff, the whole mouth stuffed with it, no teeth visible. Sher shrank back but the doctor came after him, tapping Sher's chest with one bony gloved finger. The tapping was horrible, but what was wrong with it? Sher suddenly realised that his chest was empty. I am a hollow man, he thought, and the desire to escape from Prettyman's intrusive finger became overwhelming. He struggled to call Val, to cry out, found himself unable to do so. Pull free, he thought, pull free. Suddenly he was awake.

There was knocking on the door. The time was seven forty-five. The first thought that occurred to him was that breakfast had been brought too early. Then he woke Val, and opened the door. Jimmy stood there, his face the colour of milk, his eyes frightened. 'The PM,' he said. 'He's dead.'

In Decker's bedroom they found Prettyman in pyjamas

and dressing gown. His jaw was bluer than ever, and he was chewing rhythmically, although no white stuff came from his mouth. He told them briefly what had happened. The doctor had suggested an insulin injection before Decker went to bed, but the Prime Minister had said he felt fine, and had eaten and drunk carefully during the evening. 'That was when my eye was on him. I'd been watching him, and I saw no sign of tiredness. It's quite true that if he'd been eating and drinking carefully he shouldn't have needed an injection. We'd reached a point where he was having them only three times weekly instead of every day, and once a satisfactory blood sugar level had been reached we could have tapered off to just one injection a week, always providing he kept to his diet. But he was one of those patients who deliberately deceive you, perhaps deceive themselves as well. Stupid, stupid.' It was hard to know whether he referred to Decker or himself.

Decker was an early riser. Jimmy had come to call him at six o'clock as usual, and found him on the floor unconscious. He had vomited, and was in a diabetic coma. The doctor had injected him then with a full dose of insulin, but it was too late. He had died an hour later.

Sher asked why he had not been taken to hospital. Doctor Prettyman stopped chewing for a moment.

'Because I knew exactly what had happened, had given him the only possible treatment, and the nearest hospital is more than twenty miles away.'

'It seems strange that he didn't call you after he vomited.'

'Not at all. He would have felt very weak, and been no more than semi-conscious. He must have tried to get back to bed and then collapsed, so that Jimmy found him on the floor.'

'May I see him?'

'If you want to.' The doctor lifted the sheet. Decker's face was peaceful, the eyes had been closed.

'Where did you give the injection?'

Prettyman again stopped chewing, stared at Sher. 'I

know you play a detective on the box, but don't think you can bring your play acting into real life. You want to see the injection? Right.' He pulled down the sheet, turned over the body which was clothed only in a pyjama jacket, and pointed to the needle marks on the left buttock. 'If you've got any medical knowledge at all you'll see they're recent. And you can see older marks of other injections. Go on, look.' The older puncture marks were clearly visible. 'Satisfied?'

Sher pulled back the sheet. 'You'll be happy to sign the death certificate?'

The doctor's voice had in it a growl of anger. 'I won't be *happy* to sign it, because if he'd taken proper care of himself it could have been prevented, but I'll sign it, yes.' With the sheet replaced his manner became less aggressive. 'I told you I was worried about him, this could have happened at any time. He hated the idea of injections, prided himself on always being fit.' He shook his head. 'I must get dressed.'

When they were back in their room Sher said, 'I don't believe it, I don't believe what he was saying about Decker not taking proper care of himself. There's something wrong.' He paused with one sock on, the other in his hand, looking at the wall.

'He was careful when we were with him, but you know what Prettyman said about the Princess who gorged in secret, I suppose he was like that. It's sad, he was fun.'

'He admired you.'

'He had taste,' Val said complacently. 'And he was a good host. Last night he really encouraged that little man, Josh whatever his name is, he was tongue-tied at first and then the PM started asking questions about sport and he was away, with all that stuff about cricket poems and Hornby and Barlow. I believe he could have recited the whole of the Joan Hunter Dunn poem if we'd asked. What's the matter?'

'Barlow, of course, that's what I was trying to think of.'

'Josh said he was an opening batsman, played for Lancashire, what's he got to do with it?'

'Nothing.' Sher stood up. At moments of excitement, like this one, his gaze had an intensity that could not have been bettered by the genuine Sherlock. 'This was Kenneth Barlow. Some time in the Fifties he murdered his wife by giving her an injection of insulin.'

'You mean she had diabetes, and he gave her too much?'

'No. She didn't have diabetes. That was the point.' Val stared at him, uncomprehending. 'Insulin keeps the blood sugar level if you're a diabetic, and you stay healthy as long as you observe a reasonable diet. But supposing you're not a diabetic, a powerful insulin injection will send you into a coma. That's just what Barlow did. Then after his wife had gone into coma he made sure of killing her by putting her in a bath and pushing her head under water.'

'But Decker did have diabetes, he told us so himself.'

'And who diagnosed it? Doctor Prettyman. Decker believed what he was told, obeyed doctor's orders about his diet – we only have Prettyman's word for it that he was a secret eater and drinker, everything we saw suggested the contrary. He submitted to injections that were either placebos or perhaps something that induced the thirst that's one symptom of diabetes. Then last night Prettyman gave him a lethal injection *before* going over to Waymark's suite, not after he'd collapsed. After that all he had to do was wait for Jimmy to call him with the news that Decker was in a coma.'

'That sounds terribly cold blooded.'

'Does Prettyman strike you as a warm blooded man?'

'But why would he do it?'

'Why Prettyman should want Decker dead I don't know, but it must have a connection with Waymark.'

'And it's pure theory, you don't have a single fact to base it on.'

'Wrong, there's one very hard fact. Doctor Langer of the University of Groningen doesn't exist. And since he doesn't exist—' He left the sentence unfinished, stared into space.

'I'm going to call up Brinsley and ask him to come over and examine the body with a view to an autopsy which will show if Decker really was a diabetic.'

'Do you think he'll come?'

'I'm sure he wouldn't miss it.' When he put down the telephone he was smiling. 'As I thought, Brinsley's delighted to have the chance of playing medical detective. He'll be here in an hour or less. Now let's tell our gum-chewing doctor and see his reaction.'

There was a knock on the door, and the girl who had served at dinner appeared, carrying a tray. Sher looked at his watch, and saw with astonishment that the time was precisely eight thirty.

'Paul liked efficiency,' Val said. 'He'd have been pleased his death hasn't impaired the staff service. Do you know, I'm terribly hungry. Could you delay your confrontation with Doctor Bluejaw until after breakfast?'

The orange juice was fresh, the croissants warm, the coffee strong. Sher was finishing his second cup when the telephone beside the bed rang. Val answered it, and said they would be along in a couple of minutes.

'That was check it first with Mr Hurst. He presumed we knew of the tragic event, and could he speak to us. I said he could.'

They found Hurst in the office he had indicated to them when, only two weeks but as it seemed a very long time ago, he had escorted them from the great hall to Decker's suite. He sat behind a large desk with three telephones on it, wearing what looked like the same blue suit with faint pinstripe in which they had first seen him, the same white shirt and blue tie. Did the pale eyes look more anxious than they had done last night? His first words, spoken in a voice even more subdued than usual, had something comic about them.

'I understand that you know of the tragically sudden death of the Prime Minister.' Sher said yes. 'From a purely practical point of view, I'm fortunately able to deal with everything at present on hand, but you can understand that considerable distress has been caused to Mr Waymark. He was used to dealing with the Prime Minister, and is at present in what the doctor calls a state of shock.'

'You mean Doctor Prettyman has sedated him?'

'I think that may be the case.' He peered at Sher over his glasses, the lowered voice dropped almost to a whisper. 'In the circumstances the doctor advises that it would be most inadvisable for him to attend the reading you so kindly arranged to give. I am sure you will agree that cancellation is inevitable in the circumstances. Of course your fee will be paid just as if the reading had been given.'

'I don't believe you.' Hurst looked astonished. 'I don't believe he'd want to cancel the reading. I want to see him.'

'Quite impossible.' He rose in alarm as Sher got up and made for the door. Val, a dutiful wife, followed him. They saw Hurst reach for one of the telephones on his desk as they left the room.

They went along the corridor, through the green baize door. In the gloom of Waymark's apartment the tall figure of Doctor Prettyman barred their way.

'The Mogul is in a state of shock,' he said. 'He must on no account be disturbed.'

Sher said, 'Prettyman, I know what happened. I know how Decker died.' The doctor had been chewing. Now he stopped, stared at Sher. 'A specialist will be here within an hour to examine the body, and you know what he'll find as well as I do. If I were you I should get out while you've got the chance. Now, I'm going in to see Waymark.'

'You're too late,' Prettyman said, but he made no attempt to stop Sher as the actor pushed past him. The sitting room was empty, the curtains drawn. Sher opened the door of the bedroom, and went in. As Val followed him she gave a quick involuntary gasp, fearful of what she might find.

The bedroom was in almost complete darkness. The bed was made, but there was nobody in it. Sher stared at the sheets, then struck his forehead. 'Of course. What a fool I've been.'

'Even in her bewilderment Val could not refrain from wondering what Sherlock Holmes story he had taken the phrase from. Back in the sitting room Sher went to the window, pulled the curtain cord. 'Waymark knew it.'

'Knew what?'

'Knew he'd be going out this morning to get the manuscript. That's why he showed so little interest when I said I had to be present, because he'd already arranged to go to the meeting without me. But who arranged it, who did he go with? I'll look in Prettyman's room, you see if you can find him.' She returned two or three minutes later, shaking her head. 'I don't see any sign of Hurst either. At least, he's not in his office.'

'The chances are they know the game's up, they're both on the run.'

'What game?'

He seemed not to hear her. 'Nothing in Prettyman's room to say where Waymark went, or who with. They had to get him away.' She started to say she could not see why, when he snapped his fingers. 'Polly Flinders. Come on.'

They found Polly in her room at the residential complex filing her nails, her bags ready packed. Sher asked why she was leaving.

'Now the PM's dead they want to say goodbye Polly. That's all right by me.'

'Polly, why would they do that? It's the Mogul you talk to, not the PM.' She shrugged. 'Why do you think the PM died?'

'Cause he had diabetes, didn't look after himself, ate the wrong stuff, things like that. Coulda happened any time, Doc Prettyman told me.'

'He didn't die of diabetes. He was murdered.'

'Murdered? Get away.' But there was a flare of fear in her eyes.

'Now they're going to kill Waymark, and you're helping them. You'll be an accessory, Polly, because you sent him off.'

'I never, that's a bloody lie. All I did was take a message.'

'What message?'

'He wanted to have this meet, didn't he, something to do with that Sherlock Holmes stuff. He didn't want the PM or anyone to know, so I just gave him the message, that's all.'

'What message, Polly?' She stayed silent. Val watched in astonishment as Sher, her good conventional husband, shook the girl's shoulders, slapped her face and shouted, 'You stupid girl, *what message?*'

The slap, not a hard one, seemed to convince Polly that the questioning was serious. 'About how he'd be collected and taken to the meet.'

'Who was collecting him?' He looked again at the cases, and knew. 'It was the Gate Officer, Brian Watson. And you're waiting for him to come back, you're going away with him. Right, isn't that right?' She nodded. 'What did he tell you?'

'Just there'd be a lot of money in it for us. We're going to Spain, a villa, near Torremolinos but not there, Brian says it's got no class. This villa's got class, all the bedrooms en suite. It's real, I've seen the tickets. Brian says we won't come back.'

'You won't get there. Where was it?'

'Where was what?' She said defiantly, 'You're bleeding threatening me all the time, why should I tell you?'

'Let me,' Val said. She spoke to the girl. 'Polly, we think the Mogul's life is in danger, and if anything happens to him you and Brian will both be in bad trouble. So tell us where Brian was taking him for the meeting.'

'It was the three—' At this point her voice broke, and she wailed the rest of it, '—jolly gentlemen.'

'You mean he was meeting three—'

'Not meeting them, no, you stupid sods, it's a *pub*. On the moor, near Buckfastleigh. My Gawd, do you really think I'm in trouble? All I did was give Warry a message.'

'And help to get Lavender sacked,' Sher said. She stared at him. He spoke to Val. 'You stay here, look after her, wait for Brinsley.' She began to protest, say she wanted to go with him. 'Be quiet, Val, you're more use here. I'm going after Waymark. I hope it's not too late.' Too late for what, she wanted to ask, but he was at the door. There he turned and said, 'You were right all the time, you know that?'

What, she wondered, had she been right about?

In Sher's recollection the drive across the moor seemed to have taken hours. He found himself after a quarter of a mile confronted by a typical Dartmoor mist, so thick in places that one could see no more than a few yards, then clearing completely only to surround the car after another couple of hundred yards, with the clinging ectoplasmic intensity of the stuff that had come out of Prettyman's mouth in the dream. These alternations of mist and clarity gave an air of unreality to the landscape. The typical scenery of the moor does not vary greatly to the unexpert eye, and now it seemed to Sher that he saw the same bushes and bits of scrub he had passed five minutes earlier. The moor roads are for the most part straight, but he had taken a left turn that said 'Buckfastleigh 7' and this seemed to wind back on itself and to be remarkably similar to the road on which he had set out, so that he feared he might suddenly see the towers and drawbridge of Castle Baskerville again. Then he came to a crossroads that relieved one of his worries, because this confluence of roads was certainly new to him. On the other hand none of the signposts pointed to Buckfastleigh.

He stopped the car, looked again at his map, but was quite unable to see where he was. The signpost said variously 'Utter $1/2$', 'Nonemis $11/2$', 'Tuttlehampton 4', 'Rennell 2'.

It seemed that he had come from the direction of Tuttle-hampton although he had not passed through it. Now he chose the road to Utter, chiefly because it was nearest, and in the hope that there would be a village pub. It proved a bad choice. After driving more than a mile he had seen no village, let alone a pub. The mist remained thick in places, then cleared to show patches of moor, with an occasional glimpse of ponies. He must be well past Utter, which had perhaps been down an unsignposted road to the right, and suddenly he almost ran down a hiker who appeared in the mist, striding along in the middle of the narrow road. The hiker had a large pack on his back, wore shorts, and carried a stick. When he turned he revealed a bald head, bushy eyebrows, a red face with a small moustache. He said angrily, 'You could have run me down.'

Sher stifled his inclination to reply that a walker should not be in the middle of the road. He got out of the car and said he was sorry. The hiker tapped the BMW's bonnet with his stick.

'The motor car's a killer, you're in charge of a death machine.' He paused for a reply, and when none came continued. 'Did you ever hear of a man on foot running down a man in a death machine? Never. You kill us, we don't kill you.'

'Look, I'm sorry. Can you help me, I'm lost.'

'I'm not.'

'Can you tell me, am I near Buckfastleigh?'

'Not far. Stayed there myself last night.'

'Then perhaps you know a pub called the Three Jolly Gentlemen. That's what I'm looking for.'

'You are?' Below the small moustache a small mouth smirked.

'Do you know it?'

The hiker stared at him as if uncertain of the answer. Then he smirked again. 'I do.' Another tap on the car's bonnet. 'Take your death machine on another half mile, you'll see a left turn posted to Flyte. Your pub's a couple of hundred yards down there.'

'Many thanks.' Sher got back in the car, started the engine.

'Tell you what, ask the landlord to give you a drink on me, Jerry Hagen. You'll like the taste.' He raised his stick, left the road, and set out on a path across the moor.

Sher took the left turn. When he did so, as though at a signal, the mist thickened again. He crawled along at ten miles an hour until he saw across the road a post leaning at an angle. Above it there was a faded, almost illegible sign. He cut the engine, got out of the car, looked up and saw two figures with raised tankards. The third figure had disappeared because, as he saw now, the sign was broken. Beneath the two remaining faded figures was the legend 'Three Jolly'. A few yards back from the road stood the remains of the pub, a once-solid structure in grey stone, the windows broken, part of the roof gone. Sher thought he had been tricked – and, gallingly, by Polly – but then saw the nose of a car standing just beside the corner of a wall, in what had no doubt been at one time the pub's parking area.

He stood beside his own car listening, but heard nothing. The pub's front door was slightly open. He walked to it, stepped inside and found himself in what had been the public bar, the saloon bar to his right. The ceiling was down, empty bottles and dried excrement mixed with the trampled plaster on the floor showed that the place had been used by tramps or hikers. Now he heard voices, somewhere at the back of the pub. He went through into the saloon, and almost fell as his foot went through a floorboard soft as putty.

At the other end of the room a figure appeared. It was the Gate Officer Brian. He stood slightly crouched, blue Colt .38 police special in his right hand. He straightened up when he saw Sher and waved the gun to indicate he should come forward, then stood aside to let him pass.

The back room he entered was in a slightly better state than the front of the pub. The walls were covered with graffiti, and bottles and cans were stacked in a corner, but the flooring seemed sound, and although the ceiling showed its lath and plaster, only fragments of it had fallen. An old deal table stood in the middle of the room, and a mattress was in one corner. The room's windows had been boarded, and the only light came through the open door to the back of the pub. It was without surprise that Sher saw Jonty Johnson slumped on the mattress. He looked up as Sher came in, then quickly down again so that only the top of his head was visible, a few strands of hair covering it. Alvaro Higgins sat on the deal table, swinging his legs. Brian stood by the door to the saloon bar, twirling the Colt around occasionally on his index finger.

Sher said, 'Where is he?'

Higgins raised his eyebrows. Brian Watson said, 'Who?'

'Waymark. You brought him here. What's happened to him?'

Jonty made a choking sound, and pushed his head into the dirty mattress as if trying to burrow through it. Sher noticed something else in the semi-darkness of that corner, went across to look at it, and saw the leather-bound volume containing the photocopy of *The Kentish Manor Murders*. He picked it up, riffled the pages.

'He took the bait.'

'He took the bait,' Higgins agreed.

'And where is he?'

Jonty Johnson cried out. 'Before God I never realised, I never knew what was going to happen. They just said it would be playing a part, nobody would check on me, for a year they said—'

'What have they done with him, Jonty?' Jonty began to weep. 'You should have spoken to me when we met in that apartment block, then you wouldn't be in this mess.'

Jonty lifted his head. Tears coursed down his lined old face. The words he spoke had a certain incongruity with the tears. 'It was so much money, more than I'd ever had in my life. Playing a part, just for playing a part, they said he was going away for a while and nobody would know.' And indeed, even in these unpromising circumstances, sitting on an old mattress with tears running down his face, the likeness between Jonty and Waymark was obvious. They had the same cadaverous face and skeletal figure, even – as Sher recalled from the corridor meeting – the same shuffling walk. Fix Jonty up with black glasses and a pair of gloves. . .

Higgins came down from the table and tapped Sher playfully on the chest. 'Frankly you present a problem, Mr Haynes, one I had not expected. What are we going to do with you?'

He sounded more than ever like Conrad Veidt. With an assurance he did not feel Sher said, 'Nothing you can do. The game's over and you've lost. It was over as soon as I realised what had happened to Decker. He won't be quietly buried with Prettyman signing the death certificate. A doctor is there now, my brother Brinsley, examining the body, and you know what he'll find. Prettyman's cleared out, and I think Hurst has gone too. Your best hope is to let Waymark go if you're keeping him prisoner, then try to get back to Bolivia or wherever you came from, taking your cowboy gunman with you.'

Higgins ran a hand through his white hair, and spoke mildly. 'You've caused a great deal of trouble, but I don't think you're right. Whatever Prettyman may have done is no concern of mine. If the Mogul wants to call me in to look into his affairs after Decker's death, that's nobody's business except his and mine. After all, we're old friends.'

'You mean to tell me the Mogul will go along with that?'

'You think he won't do what I tell him, if the money's right?' He said jovially to the forlorn figure on the mattress, 'And the money will be right, my old dear, double what we talked about, and once we get over what someone or other called this little local difficulty, nothing to worry about.'

Jonty looked up hopefully. Higgins smiled at him. Sher said, 'Where's Waymark?'

It was Watson, the Colt held loosely in his hand, who answered. 'In the car boot. We're taking him back for burial in the Castle grounds. After all he built the damn place.' Sher began to walk towards the open door that led to the back of the pub. 'Where d'you think you're going?'

'To look in your car boot.'

'I shouldn't.'

Three things happened, almost together. There was a noise outside, perhaps a car door slamming. Higgins said something, the words unclear. And Sher received a great slap on the back, then his throat was stung by a bee. A slap on the back, he thought, extraordinary, Alvaro being friendly. He began to turn, to say it was no use trying to stop him, he was going to look in the car boot, but suddenly his legs had no strength in them, the bee sting felt uncommonly warm and, looking down, he saw with astonishment blood dripping down on the floor. I've been shot, he thought, Sherlock Holmes has been shot. Then there was a rush of noise, and after that blackness.

Afterwards

He opened his eyes. Brinsley was looking down on him, face disturbingly close, large nose slightly reddened, characteristic self-satisfied look on his face. A bad dream, evidently. His eyes closed again.

And opened. Five minutes, a day, a week later? He had no idea. This time he took in his surroundings, lying on a bed, evidently in a hospital room, large window, flowers and a lot of cards on a table near the bed. A tube in his nose, tiresome. He found it impossibly difficult to stay awake.

Eyes open *again*, and again there was Brinsley. His voice was rich, deep, a kind of parody of Sher's own.

'A damned near-run thing, old fellow, I can tell you. Who was it said that, Pitt or Wellington, never can remember. Bullet just a few inches to the left and you'd have been a goner, and the other one that nicked your throat, affected the vocal chords, you won't be performing on the boards again for a while, no use trying to talk.' Of course he did then attempt to speak. Only a thin unintelligible croak emerged. 'Not to worry, it will come back, the worst is over, patience is the word. You were crazy to go off like that on your own, don't know what you thought you were doing. As soon as I examined the PM's body I realised he'd been deliberately poisoned, callous devil that American doctor. I called the police at once, fortunately the Superintendent's an old friend, and he took it seriously. Lucky too that you got lost on the moor, if you'd got there earlier we'd have had two corpses to deal with instead of one. They'd stuffed the Mogul in the car boot, going to bury him in the Castle grounds where no one would ever look for the body, then replace him with what's-his-name, the actor fellow. You might like to see the papers, quite a splash.'

He held up daily papers, including a couple of tabloids which showed Brinsley smirking triumphantly outside the ruined pub. One headline said 'Devon Doctor Solves Castle Baskerville Mystery', another 'Doctor Saves Brother "Sherlock"'. Below he saw '"How I Saved My Actor Brother" by Dr Brinsley Haynes', and read a line or two: '. . . a brief examination of Decker's body convinced me that the death was not natural, and I instantly recalled the case of Kenneth Barlow . . .' But it was I who mentioned the name of Barlow when I rang you, he tried to say, all you did was confirm my suspicions. Only incoherent sounds came out. Brinsley beamed. 'Shows there's more than one detective in the family. And one who doesn't get himself shot.'

It was intolerable. He closed his eyes again.

'I've been to see you a dozen times,' Val said. 'But you were so dopey you didn't seem to understand anything I was saying. Brinsley's been looking after you marvellously. No use glaring like that, you might not be here at all if it weren't for Brinsley. And he says your voice will be all right, you just have to be patient, you'll soon be able to talk.'

He said with great effort, 'Can talk.' He was certainly much better, able to get up and sit around in a dressing gown. He had been told he could go home in a week.

'But you shouldn't. And Brinsley says I'm not to smoke when you're around. I should think if I can make that sacrifice you ought to be able to keep silent. I'll tell you what's been happening and what I've worked out, and you say if I'm right, okay? Nod or shake your head, and if you have to, write things down on this pad. First of all they've caught Langer, and he's admitted writing the manuscripts. His name's really Schultz, and he's a professional con man who specialises in forgery. Don't know exactly what they'll charge him with, he says he produced the manuscript as a commission for Higgins, wasn't trying to deceive anybody, except maybe you. He doesn't have any special interest in Sherlock Holmes, just took a course in him by reading the books, then produced his unfinished story. Just shows how easy it is, though of course you should have known it was a fake from the title.' And you'll forbear from saying *I told you so*, Sher thought as he nodded.*

'And next, Higgins. You realised he was Van Helder?' He nodded again. 'You say that now, but I wonder if it's true? He'd had a face job, and that white hair was a wig. I should have thought you'd have spotted it, but then you didn't recognise that little man Bogan when he took his wig off, so I suppose it's not surprising.' He made protesting sounds. 'Yes, I know it's different, but still. You must have got round to Higgins being Van Helder pretty late in the day.'

He wrote on the pad: *When I realised Jonty Johnson was meant to take Waymark's place.*

'That's why you said I was right all along, because I'd suggested Waymark might be dead, and someone else was in his place? Seems the idea came to Van Helder when he saw Johnson in some cabaret show in Germany and realised he looked like Waymark. I remember Marty saying Van Helder was great at planning ingenious schemes, but not strong on the details. But it could have worked. Very few people saw Waymark, so if he could get rid of Decker and effect the substitution he'd be home and dry, that was the idea. He'd

---

*Val was right about the Sherlock Holmes titles. In the whole *oeuvre* the word 'murder' is never used in the title of a novel or short story.

been trying for a long time to get his own people into the Castle and play the same trick on Decker that had been played on him. Hurst was Van Helder's man, had been all along, and he made the appointments. Decker should have got rid of him. I'm afraid the PM, much though I liked him, was really a bit naive. Of course Hurst okayed the appointment of Prettyman. Then they got Polly Flinders in, and she helped get Lavender out. Lavender was on the level and it would have been awkward to have him around, so Prettyman planted drugs on him, right?' He nodded. 'When did you work that out?'

He wrote: *At the dinner party when Prettyman pressed too hard about the diabetes, and then after Decker died.*

She said, 'You were clever but a bit slow. It was quite a simple plot really, wasn't it? Crazy but simple. And all the flummery about the Sherlock manuscript was just to get Waymark out of the Castle?' He wanted to protest against 'flummery', but couldn't. 'But I still don't understand it. Prettyman was prepared to kill Decker, why not give Waymark a dose of something or other that would send him into the next world? Why bother to get him off the premises so that he could be killed by that young thug Brian – who turns out to have a record as long as your arm by the way. Why are you shaking your head?'

He wrote: *Decker death meant to be natural.*

'And Prettyman thought there'd be no trouble?'

But for ME would have been no trouble, he wrote. *Decker dead, pension off Jimmy, Lavender and Malby sacked, nobody else cared. But VERY risky if Waymark died too, bound to be trouble. With substitution nobody would know.*

She read this with corrugated brow. 'But even so—'

Two deaths suspicious. Death of Decker accepted as natural, Waymark calls back Van H. also quite natural, nothing to arouse suspicion.

'It's a pity you can't talk,' Val said. 'You'd make it sound more credible, the need for the Sherlock forgery. But I suppose Van Helder was just too clever for his own good, loved the elaboration.' He nodded. 'Your Inspector Jansson wants him for drug offences, by the way, he may be deported. Now I'll tell you something funny. The Mogul had made a will. Guess who he left all his money to? The Sherlock Holmes Society.' Sher raised eloquent Sherlockian eyebrows. 'That's not the funny part. I still think the PM was terribly nice, but he certainly wasn't very clever. When George Darnley, the lawyer who handled all the Waymark affairs, heard Paul was dead he vanished. Whereabouts unknown, somewhere in South America that has no extradition treaty with Britain is suspected. It seems he'd been keeping a small stable of ladies and another of racehorses, and playing the markets unsuccessfully too. The accountants are burrowing into it all now, but it looks as if Waymark Enterprises may be bankrupt.'

With much effort Sher spoke. 'One thing estate could give Society.'

'*Stop talking*,' Val cried. 'What could they give the Sherlock Holmes Society? Write it down.'

Sher wrote: *The Kentish Manor Murders.*

FOR THE BEST IN PAPERBACKS, LOOK FOR THE

In every corner of the world, on every subject under the sun, Penguin represents quality and variety—the very best in publishing today.

For complete information about books available from Penguin— including Pelicans, Puffins, Peregrines, and Penguin Classics—and how to order them, write to us at the appropriate address below. Please note that for copyright reasons the selection of books varies from country to country.

In the United Kingdom: For a complete list of books available from Penguin in the U.K., please write to *Dept E.P., Penguin Books Ltd, Harmondsworth, Middlesex, UB7 0DA*.

In the United States: For a complete list of books available from Penguin in the U.S., please write to *Dept BA, Penguin*, Box 999, Bergenfield, New Jersey 07621-0999.

In Canada: For a complete list of books available from Penguin in Canada, please write to *Penguin Books Canada Ltd, 2801 John Street, Markham, Ontario L3R 1B4*.

In Australia: For a complete list of books available from Penguin in Australia, please write to the *Marketing Department, Penguin Books Australia Ltd, P.O. Box 257, Ringwood, Victoria 3134*.

In New Zealand: For a complete list of books available from Penguin in New Zealand, please write to the *Marketing Department, Penguin Books (NZ) Ltd, Private Bag, Takapuna, Auckland 9*.

In India: For a complete list of books available from Penguin, please write to *Penguin Overseas Ltd, 706 Eros Apartments, 56 Nehru Place, New Delhi, 110019*.

In Holland: For a complete list of books available from Penguin in Holland, please write to *Penguin Books Nederland B.V., Postbus 195, NL–1380AD Weesp, Netherlands*.

In Germany: For a complete list of books available from Penguin, please write to *Penguin Books Ltd, Friedrichstrasse 10–12, D–6000 Frankfurt Main 1, Federal Republic of Germany*.

In Spain: For a complete list of books available from Penguin in Spain, please write to *Longman Penguin España, Calle San Nicolas 15, E–28013 Madrid, Spain*.

In Japan: For a complete list of books available from Penguin in Japan, please write to *Longman Penguin Japan Co Ltd, Yamaguchi Building, 2-12-9 Kanda Jimbocho, Chiyuoda-Ku, Tokyo 101, Japan*.